"You think you know me that well?"

Lucy glared at him in what had become a stare down. "You have an overabundance of confidence. You know who you are and what you want."

"Then you should know I want you for more than just a friend," he countered. Lucy laughed, the sound making him more uncomfortable with each passing second. "What's so funny?"

"You, Calum. I knew you wanted to be more than a friend when you offered to go with me to Furever Paws to foster a dog. Then it was the visits to the vet. And lately it's sending me lunch, which I truly love and appreciate."

"Well, damn," Calum said under his breath. "I thought I was being subtle."

"Subtlety happens not to be one of your strong suits, handsome."

"Miss Tucker, are you flirting with me?"

A hint of a smile lifted the corners of her sexy mouth. "Yes, I am, Mr. Ramsey. Does that bother you?"

Dear Reader,

When I was invited to contribute to the Furever Yours continuity, it was a blessing for me because months earlier I had put down Oliver, my beloved Yorkshire terrier who had been my constant companion for more than thirteen years. Oliver had the heart of a lion in his five-pound body but the sweetness of Buttercup, a pregnant golden retriever. As I began writing *The Bookshop Rescue*, I found healing and accepted that my fur baby is now in a better place.

It has taken bookstore owner Lucy Tucker a while to realize Buttercup isn't the only one who needs rescuing. The dog becomes her therapist when she can tell her four-legged foster her innermost secrets—and that includes her attraction to the owner of the bowling alley. Lucy has loved and lost, and she has no intention of trusting a man or a woman again—even if that man is nothing like her ex-fiancé.

Calum Ramsey, the owner of Pins and Pints, is of the belief that helping Lucy lift heavy boxes of books and accompanying her when she must take Buttercup to the vet is what supportive business owners do for each other. Although Lucy is unlike any other woman he has ever known, Calum knows he is not ready for marriage or willing to start a family because of his own turbulent childhood. However, the night Buttercup goes into labor and delivers five puppies will change Calum and Lucy, while their world as they know it will never be the same.

Of course, it is Buttercup and her five adorable puppies, Waffle, Grits, Beignet, Fritter and Pancake, who will tug at your heart as Lucy and Calum rescue a love that promises forever. I hope you will enjoy *The Bookshop Rescue* as much as I enjoyed writing it.

Happy reading!

Rochelle Alers

The Bookshop Rescue

ROCHELLE ALERS

HARLEQUIN

SPECIAL
EDITION

Special thanks and acknowledgment are given to Rochelle Alers for her contribution to the Furever Yours miniseries.

HARLEQUIN®
SPECIAL
EDITION™

Recycling programs for this product may not exist in your area.

ISBN-13: 978-1-335-40854-9

The Bookshop Rescue

Harlequin Enterprises ULC
22 Adelaide St. West, 41st Floor
Toronto, Ontario M5H 4E3, Canada
www.Harlequin.com

Printed in U.S.A.

Since 1988, nationally bestselling author **Rochelle Alers** has written more than eighty books and short stories. She has earned numerous honors, including the Zora Neale Hurston Award, the Vivian Stephens Award for Excellence in Romance Writing and a Career Achievement Award from *RT Book Reviews*. She is a member of Zeta Phi Beta Sorority, Inc., Iota Theta Zeta Chapter. A full-time writer, she lives in a charming hamlet on Long Island. Rochelle can be contacted through her website, www.rochellealers.org.

Books by Rochelle Alers

Harlequin Special Edition

Bainbridge House

A New Foundation
Christmas at the Chateau

Wickham Falls Weddings

Home to Wickham Falls
Her Wickham Falls SEAL
The Sheriff of Wickham Falls
Dealmaker, Heartbreaker
This Time for Keeps
Second-Chance Sweet Shop

American Heroes

Claiming the Captain's Baby
Twins for the Soldier

Visit the Author Profile page
at Harlequin.com for more titles.

To Oliver—I miss you, baby boy.

Chapter One

Pinpoints of color from late-afternoon sunlight shimmered through the Frank Lloyd Wright–inspired patterned beveled glass on Chapter One's solid oak door as Lucy Tucker locked it and flipped the sign over to "Closed."

Since fostering a pregnant rescue golden retriever from the Furever Paws Animal Rescue, she'd made it a practice to go directly home after closing for the day on the days when she didn't bring Buttercup to the bookstore. But the gentle canine was with her today, resting on her bed in the rear office, so Lucy decided to take the time to change her display window.

She picked up a book on gardening and positioned it in the window display with several cookbooks on grilling, smoking meat, the perfect picnic and entertaining. Then she set out several books featuring ideas for Mother's Day. It was early May in Spring Forest and, with warmer temperatures, the titles on display celebrated the spring and coming summer months.

Lucy was proud of her storefront. She'd meticulously review stacks of books, searching for ones she felt would catch the eye of anyone passing by. She went all-out for Halloween, Thanksgiving and Christmas, when she decorated the window with holiday-themed books and colorful miniatures of houses, stores, cars and people.

Her first Christmas display had been highly successful with young children. They'd stood outside the bookstore, transfixed by the rotating snow globes in the center of a winter wonderland of a miniature town.

Owning and operating her own business had only become a reality after Lucy, at twenty-six, resigned her position as a Charlotte elementary schoolteacher. Remaining in her hometown had not been an option for her after her fiancé had run off with her best friend/maid of honor a month before their wedding. Lucy had known she couldn't continue to live in a place where she would inevitably run into the newlyweds on a regular basis.

Fortunately, she was able to get a refund of ninety percent of the deposit for her wedding expenses, plus the money she got for selling her engagement ring. It was enough to start fresh in Spring Forest, a suburb of Raleigh that was more than one hundred and fifty miles from Charlotte.

While it was a comfort to be away from people who knew about her past, she couldn't escape her own emotional scars. Even after more than a year, she still struggled to come to terms with the betrayal from Danielle—someone she had always thought of as her sister. It had completely shattered Lucy's ability to trust other people. She struggled to make new friends and absolutely refused to consider dating again—so she ended up throwing herself into work.

When she'd first moved to Spring Forest and seen the vacant storefront in the historic downtown area, she'd known it would be the perfect location for a new bookstore. She'd poured all her heart—and all her time—into getting the store up and running, and she was proud of all she'd achieved. Just as she was proud of the display that was now…done.

She had just finished when she heard tapping on the window. Calum Ramsey, the owner of the bowling alley next door—Pins and Pints—motioned for her to unlock the door. Smiling and nodding, she went to the door.

Lucy had initially met Calum when she'd walked into the bowling alley to introduce herself as his new business neighbor. When she'd told him she projected opening within a month once all the shelves were installed, she'd found herself mesmerized by his intense stare. To her relief, his gaze wasn't lecherous, but rather curious. Curious as to who she was and why she had moved to Spring Forest. If Calum had been intrigued with her, then it was the same with Lucy. The owner of the bowling alley was a trifecta: tall, dark and incredibly attractive—something she'd been unable to ignore during their subsequent encounters, no matter how hard she tried. She didn't want to date, didn't want to fall in love—never wanted to be that gullible again. But man, he made it hard to keep her attraction in check.

Although it had been a year since their initial introduction, there were occasions when she still found her reactions to Calum vaguely disturbing. Whenever he volunteered to move merchandise for her, Lucy forced herself not to ogle the rippling muscles in his biceps or how the fabric in his slim-cut jeans strained against muscular thighs whenever he bent down to pick up boxes of books. But as deeply drawn she'd found herself to Calum, she knew nothing would come of it because she refused to become involved with another man.

Lucy opened the door, a tentative smile lifting the corners of her mouth as she took in Calum's cropped dark hair, neatly trimmed goatee and large, light-brown eyes. She took a deep breath to steady her runaway pulse as he walked in, the familiar scent of his cologne wafting to her nostrils.

"Is Buttercup okay?" Calum asked.

"Yes. Why did you ask?"

"I came by earlier this afternoon and Miss Grace told me you had gone home to get something for Buttercup."

She knew Calum's concern for Buttercup was genuine. He'd gone with her to pick up the dog from Furever Paws after Buttercup and many others had been rescued from a backyard breeder.

The decision to foster Buttercup until she could be adopted had been a win-win for Lucy. Her bookstore was successful, but after a year of devoting all her time to it, she was lonely. When she'd mentioned to Calum that she'd wanted to foster one of the rescues, he'd offered to accompany her to select a dog.

The instant she'd seen the pregnant golden retriever, Lucy had claimed her, agreeing to foster Buttercup until she weaned her puppies. Calum had been the one to carry the heartbreakingly underweight one-year-old dog to his SUV.

"I had to go home and get more food for Buttercup. She needs to eat smaller meals throughout the day."

Calum nodded, smiling. "It's great that she's getting back to a healthy weight. I wish I could come visit her more, but I've been tied up organizing the summer bowling leagues."

"You need an assistant, Calum. You can't do it all. When I first opened the bookstore, it was impossible for me to take care of the register *and* help customers find the books they're looking for, so that's when I advertised for two part-time assistants."

"I know, Lucy. I keep telling myself I need to advertise for one, then something comes up and I forget about it until the next mini crisis. Now, back to Buttercup. How is she?"

"Her belly is getting nice and round," Lucy said, voice filled with pride.

"That's because she's living the high life."

Lucy laughed. "It's because she's really spoiled."

Calum's eyebrows lifted slightly as he crossed muscular arms over a broad chest. "Now I wonder just who spoiled her."

She dropped her gaze. "Guilty as charged." Lucy wanted to tell him that spoiling Buttercup was the least she could do after what the canine had endured at the puppy mill.

"I really like Buttercup."

Lucy sobered. "So do I. I really don't want to think of the time when her pups are weaned and they will all leave to be adopted."

"That's why you foster, Lucy—to get them ready to be adopted out."

She'd grown so attached to the golden retriever that she'd seriously thought about adopting her. However, when she'd signed on to foster a dog, she was aware it was temporary and that someone else may want to adopt Buttercup.

"I know, but it's not going to be easy letting her go. I hope I don't lose it and start bawling. And let me warn you that I cry ugly."

"I doubt it will come to that, Lucy."

"You don't want to be around when that time comes, Calum." Lucy knew she had to psych herself up for the inevitable. That once Buttercup weaned her puppies, they would no longer be her responsibility. They would go to their forever homes. And she'd be left behind.

Calum stroked his goatee with a forefinger, grinning affectionately when Lucy mentioned crying ugly. Even with red and swollen eyes, he would still find her stunningly gorgeous.

When Lucy Tucker had first walked into his bowling alley more than a year ago, he'd found himself doing a lot of volunteering for the tall and curvy woman who occasionally kept him from a restful night's sleep. However, as he'd gotten to see more of her, he'd realized she was the type of woman a man married and settled down with.

At thirty, Calum had had his share of relationships, abruptly ending them whenever the subject of marriage and children was mentioned. It was different with Lucy because not once had she indicated she wanted more than friendship, which he found refreshing. And their friendship extended to his willingness to lift boxes of books and/or accepting deliveries whenever the bookstore was closed.

Calum's gaze took in everything about Lucy's face. Even without makeup, she was a natural beauty. Her dark brown, chin-length, naturally wavy bob framed a flawless khaki-hued complexion radiating good health. He liked the way her dark brown eyes crinkled at the corners whenever she smiled, while he struggled not to rudely stare at her full, sensual mouth that he'd fantasized about kissing. And knowing there would never be anything more than friendship between them was a blessing in disguise for Calum. He knew without a doubt becoming romantically involved with Lucy was certain to make him forget why he wasn't the marrying kind.

"You'll do just fine, knowing Buttercup will go to a good home." He hesitated. "Maybe after Buttercup and her puppies are adopted you could ask Bethany to become a permanent foster," he said, referring to the director of Furever Paws.

Lucy sighed. "I don't know about that. It all depends on how I feel after giving up Buttercup. If I don't have a complete meltdown, then I will consider fostering another dog." She paused. "I know I haven't told you this, but I truly appreciate you helping me doing some of the heavy lifting here in the store."

"I told you before, folks in Spring Forest look out for one another. And that goes double for us in the business district. Live local, shop local isn't just an empty slogan, Lucy. We do what we have to do to keep folks coming in and our doors open."

Lucy lowered her eyes. "You're right, Calum. I have to keep reminding myself of that, but I still appreciate your help."

"Speaking of helping, I stopped by earlier because a box of yours was delivered to me while you were out. Do you want me to bring it over now?"

"Okay. And thank you again, Calum."

A slight frown furrowed his forehead. "For what?"

"For accepting my deliveries."

Leaning close, he pressed a kiss to her cheek. "Appreciation and thanks accepted." He took a step back. "I'll go and get that box now."

Calum left the bookstore and walked over to Pins and Pints. He didn't know what had possessed him to kiss Lucy. Even if it was only her cheek. He didn't want to believe he was weakening, lowering his resistance when it came to the bookshop beauty when he knew he should stay away from her.

There were days when he deliberately walked past the bookstore and he forced himself not to even look in, and then there were days when he'd slow down and wait to catch her gaze through the window before waving and moving on. But today, the shipping company had dropped off boxes that gave Calum a legitimate reason to contact Lucy.

He opened the door to Pins and Pints and was met with a rush of cool air from the newly upgraded central air-conditioning system. What had been an old-fashioned, decades-old bowling alley had undergone a massive renovation three years ago after Calum had purchased it from the original owners. The updated floor plans included a ten-lane bowling alley with the mini pin and bowling ball set up to the right of the front door, a massive mahogany bar with plenty of bar stools, and ten tables for food service. Several months ago, he'd installed a half dozen flat screens, always muted with closed captions and tuned to sports channels.

The bar offered everything from soda fountain pop to local beer on tap to a specialty cocktail. Pins and Pints also offered a small food menu with a variety of appetizers, sides and sandwiches. Freshly made popcorn was a favorite.

Once he'd decided to go into business for himself, Calum had developed a detailed business plan specifying quarterly projections for the first two years. It wasn't the life he'd imagined following his graduation from Duke University with degrees in accounting and finance. But after years in an investment bank, he'd gotten tired of making money for other people and decided he wanted to run his own business.

That's when he'd returned to Spring Forest to purchase and restore the bowling alley. He came in before nine—two hours before Pins and Pints hours of operation—and most nights he didn't leave until midnight. Fridays and Saturdays were the exception when the bowling alley closed at one in the morning.

For Calum, putting in long hours during a seven-day workweek was not conducive to dating or socializing. Whenever his friends from Raleigh or former coworkers invited him to get together, work was always his excuse. Although fully staffed, Calum knew Lucy was right about his hiring an assistant manager—someone to come in and supervise the other employees so he could take more time off. He was aware working so much was a recipe for burnout.

He found the box in a corner of the stockroom, hoisted it onto his shoulder, and retraced his steps to Chapter One. It was after six and young couples were coming in after work to bowl. When all the lanes were in use, the sound of balls hitting pins, followed by cheers or groans, never failed to make Calum smile. He nodded to a couple that had recently celebrated their engagement at Pins and Pints.

Lucy was waiting for him when he returned to Chapter One.

She'd taken off the smock and he swallowed to relieve the dryness in his throat when he stared at the outline of her full breasts under a long-sleeved, light-blue cotton tee she'd paired with jeans that hugged her curves in all the right places. Lucy Tucker was blatant temptation on two long legs.

"Where do you want me to put the box?"

"Follow me, and I'll open the office for you."

Calum stared at the gentle sway of her hips as she walked, then forced himself to look away before his appreciation became impossible to hide. It had been a long time—much too long—since he'd been that turned on. Just his luck that she had no interest in him beyond friendship.

To distract himself, he focused on the bookstore's décor. Lucy had told him once that she'd decided she wanted Chapter One to resemble a personal library with stacks of books, well-worn leather armchairs and mahogany side tables for those wishing to sit and read. Even the children's area, with child-sized chairs and tables located toward the left rear of the store, beckoned her youngest customers to come and read as their parents browsed row upon row of books. Her preference for the Art Deco era was reflected in the patterned stained glass on the front door and the door to her office. The contractor had refinished the dark wood floor and applied polyurethane until it glimmered a deep golden brown. Rather than cover the stark-white walls with photos of authors and book covers, Lucy had opted for famous quotes from various books stenciled in black calligraphy.

Calum glanced at some of those famous quotes as he walked past dark wood bookshelves, but his eyes kept getting drawn back to Lucy's voluptuous body as she unlocked the office and stepped aside to let him enter.

"You can set it on the workstation."

Calum complied, looking over to see Buttercup lying on her side on a large orthopedic dog bed in a far corner of the office. She opened her eyes, but didn't move. Lucy was right. Her exposed belly was a lot rounder than the last time he'd seen her.

"It looks as if she's had a haircut."

Lucy smiled and nodded. "Last week I took her over to Barkyard Boarding to be groomed because she was shedding all over the house. She looks great, right? So different from the rescue that I brought home from Furever Paws."

"I'll get out of your way so you can go home and take care of Buttercup. Good night." He wanted to run, not walk, out of Chapter One just to put some distance between himself and Lucy.

"Good night, Calum."

When he made it out the door, Calum swore under his breath. He hadn't had a serious relationship since college and when that had ended, he'd made a practice to stick strictly to casual dating. She couldn't know it, but Lucy was pushing him closer and closer to rethinking that self-imposed vow.

Calum had always been forthcoming when he told women he wasn't ready for marriage and/or children. Some were willing to take him at his word, while others thanked him for his honesty and a nice evening, and politely informed him that he should lose their number.

Since returning to Spring Forest, he'd told himself

he was too involved in making his business venture viable to date, but a silent voice told him he was in denial. He wanted to ask Lucy out, but he wasn't certain how to go about risking the change to their friendship.

Calum knew there was only way to find out.

And that was to ask her.

Chapter Two

Lucy opened the door and waited for Buttercup to follow her in.

"As soon as I change my clothes, I'll cuddle with you before giving you some food and clean water."

It's been said that a dog is a man's best friend, but if "man" was changed to "woman" then nothing could be truer for Lucy. Buttercup was loyal and that was a lot more than she could say for her duplicitous fiancé and so-called friend. Looking back, Lucy realized she should've noticed the amount of time Johnny and Danielle had been spending together. Even her mother had remarked on it, but Lucy had brushed it off with the excuse they were discussing her wedding plans. More like plans to *wreck* her wedding.

Not that she would have wanted him to marry her and then cheat. Lucy wasn't certain how she would've reacted if she'd found out after they'd exchanged vows. And she didn't want to be featured in one of those trashy televised true crime shows where the wife decided to mete out her own brand of justice to her cheating spouse and his lover. The elopement a month before the wedding had hurt like crazy— but at least it had been a clean break.

When life gives you lemons, make lemonade.

Her lemonade was relocating to Spring Forest to reinvent herself, opening Chapter One and renting the small three-bedroom house in the older section of Kingdom Creek. Perhaps one of these days she would feel benevolent enough to send Johnny and Danielle a large fruit basket thanking them for giving her the freedom to live her best life.

She walked into her bedroom, Buttercup following, and exchanged her tee and jeans for a pair of sweatpants and a tank top. The temperature in the room was warm, but Lucy did not turn on the window unit. She didn't like sleeping under a pile of blankets during the spring and summer months.

After she cuddled and fed Buttercup, she would wait to take her for a walk and carry out their nighttime routine before bed. When Lucy had first brought her home, she'd set Buttercup's bed in an area off the galley kitchen that doubled as the pantry and laundry room. Even when the dog whined to get into bed with her, Lucy refused. She did not want to establish a habit of having the dog sleeping in her bed.

For now, she left the bedroom, settled down on the floor in the living room, and waited for Buttercup to crawl into her lap. It wasn't easy for Lucy to cradle a dog weighing close to fifty pounds, but they made it work. Buttercup shifted into a more comfortable position and then rested her head against Lucy's chest. Smiling, Lucy gently stroked her ear.

"I know you want to hear some of the talk that floated around the bookstore today," she began as if speaking to another human. "That poor cat, Oliver, is still missing. There are posters all over town asking folks to call if they see him. I do hope they find him soon because little Brooklyn Hobbs has been very upset. She blames herself for him getting out when she forgot to close the screen door.

"And there's gossip going around that Birdie Whitaker and the old veterinarian, Doc J, are arguing about him going back to his place in Florida. Another romance on the rocks. I should take that as a warning sign, right? So why can't I stop staring at Calum Ramsey? Whenever he looks at me, I want to jump the man's bones. It would be more than embarrassing because I've told him I just want to be friends. What kind of double message would it send if I asked, 'Although we're friends, would you mind if we sleep together?' And I doubt if he would be willing to accept being a friend with benefits. Something tells me Calum isn't one to dabble with when it comes to relationships. It's either all or nothing."

Buttercup whined softly and Lucy smiled and pressed a kiss on the dog's head. "All right. Cuddle time is over, and I'll feed you now." Buttercup was not only her companion. She'd become her therapy dog, in a manner of speaking. Lucy could say anything she wanted and not have to worry about it being repeated.

Lucy got up and went into the bathroom to wash Buttercup's food and water bowl, the dog following and watching her every move. Minutes later she half filled the bowl with the high-quality puppy food the vet had recommended and set it in the elevated double-diner dog feeder, then filled the other bowl with water. Buttercup sniffed the food and turned to look at Lucy.

"You're not going to get a doggie biscuit until you eat all your food," Lucy chided softly. The golden retriever preferred the dog treats to her meals, yet she needed the nutrition for her puppies' sake.

Lucy left Buttercup to eat her dinner while she opened the refrigerator to take out a container with broiled shrimp. She'd decided to prepare a Caesar salad with the shrimp. She closed Chapter One on Sundays and on that day she handled laundry, housecleaning and cooking for the week. So much for a day of rest. Her maternal grandmother would be horrified.

Lucy smiled when she recalled her beloved Grammie for whom she'd been named. She loved listening to her grandmother talk about her childhood. She had planned to be the first woman in her family to attend college, but her dream had been deferred when her mother died. As the oldest girl, she'd had to help her dad take care of her younger siblings. However, she did live long enough see to her daughter graduate and her granddaughter start college. Lucy liked to think of how proud Grammie would be of her having a degree and owning her own business—even if it did mean doing all her housework on the Lord's day.

She had help in the store, as she'd told Calum, but it wasn't enough to give her more than the one day off when the store was closed. Her assistants only worked five hours a day, three days each. Her first hire had been Miss Evelyn Grace, a retired middle school cafeteria worker, who had answered the ad within days of it appearing in the *Spring Forest Chronicle*. A week later, Lucy hired Angela Fowler, a former school librarian and empty-nester who'd shamelessly admitted she was addicted to books.

She had a good working relationship with both women, but she wouldn't say she was close to them. Aside from Buttercup, she wasn't really close to anyone.

Lucy turned on the radio on the countertop, and opened the drawer in the refrigerator with packaged lettuce and greens. She danced around the kitchen when one of her favorite oldies started playing. Her cell phone rang as she'd begun separating romaine leaves. Recognizing the caller—the town's biweekly newspaper—she turned down the radio before putting her phone on speaker.

"Hello."

"Lucy, this is Doug, and I'm calling you from the *Spring Forest Chronicle* to let you know we were able to get your ad into our next biweekly edition. The editor has also agreed to put it on the paper's website because you are one of our regular advertisers."

She smiled to herself. "Please thank him for me." Lucy knew the local paper depended on advertising for its revenue and she advertised the bookstore in every issue.

"Will do."

She ended the call and laced her fingers together in a prayerful gesture. She hoped the ad would be the key to increasing the sale of children's books. Lucy had a dedicated reading space for children, but she planned to draw more attention to it with her Teddy Bear Storytime on Thursday nights from 7:00 p.m. to 8:00 p.m. Children aged three to five would be encouraged to wear pajamas and bring their favorite stuffed animal. In addition to the ad in the paper and on the paper's website, she planned to put up several flyers around town.

Buttercup came over to Lucy, her tail wagging. "Good girl. You finished all your food. Now you can have your treat." The dog barked at the mention of "treat." Lucy opened a ceramic jar decorated with a dog bone on the countertop and gave Buttercup a large biscuit. Holding it in her mouth, she went over to her bowl, dropped it and then picked it up again, biting off pieces until she'd devoured it completely. Lucy knew she had at least forty minutes to herself before it was time to walk Buttercup. She went back to preparing her dinner.

She sat at the kitchen table and ate the salad with shrimp, garlic-flavored croutons, shredded Parmesan and homemade Caesar dressing, and a chilled glass of lemonade. Bottled salad dressings and marinades were her pet peeves, and she'd made it a practice to concoct her own.

Buttercup was up and waiting by the time Lucy finished eating. After gathering the harness, the lead and several poop bags, they went outside as dusk was descending on Spring Forest. Lucy noticed Buttercup was walking more slowly than usual and attributed that to the growing puppies in her belly.

"Take your time, little mama. In another week or so, it all will be a memory." Lucy was both nervous and excited for the puppies to be born. Life was about to get very busy for her—she just hoped she was ready.

Calum retreated to his office, closed the door, sat behind his desk and closed his eyes. If there was such a thing as a time machine, he would get in it to go back twenty-four hours.

The vibrating of his cell phone on the bedside table had woken him an hour before sunrise, which he'd known could not be good news. And he'd been right—it was his new bartender, calling from the emergency room. He'd cut his hand on a broken glass while moonlighting as a bartender at a private event and it had taken ten sutures to close the gaping wound. Calum had told him his job was secure and he wasn't to come back to work until he was medically cleared.

He'd ended the call, tried to go back to sleep, and failed. Forty minutes later, he'd walked into Pins and Pints to the sound of running water. When he'd opened the restroom door, he'd discovered someone had blocked the sink's drain and left the faucet running. Calum had shut off the water valve, retrieved the industrial mop and bucket from the janitorial closet and mopped up most of the water. He'd locked the bathroom and placed an Out of Order sign on the door before calling the plumbing company. Then he'd called in a replacement for his missing bartender. Fortunately, the other two bartenders were more than willing to fill in because it meant extra hours and tips.

Seeing no time machine suddenly appear, Calum resolved himself to focus on his next task. He had just begun inputting the revised employee work hours into the computer to generate the payroll when he'd heard a light tapping on the door. He had a hard-

and-fast rule that he was not to be disturbed if the door was closed. Someone tapped again.

"What is it?"

The door opened slightly and Pamela the employee responsible for shoe rental, stuck her head through the opening. "There's someone here to see you."

He frowned. "Does that someone have a name?"

"He wouldn't give it to me, but he says you'll know him when you see him."

Calum was not in the mood to play guessing games. He was down one bartender for an indefinite length of time, and the plumber had had to replace the entire sink.

"Send him in." He didn't bother to disguise his annoyance. The door opened wider, and Calum pushed away from the desk and rose to his feet. The tall man in the doorway was someone he hadn't seen in years. "I don't believe it. Aiden Harding."

"Believe it, Ramsey. It's yours truly in the flesh."

Extending his hand, he came around the desk, and shook hands with his old friend and coworker from Raleigh. Aiden was the quintessential golden boy with his natural wavy blond hair and aquamarine eyes. Aiden had actually been approached by a representative from a modeling agency with an offer for him to appear in a Ralph Lauren magazine layout, but he'd declined.

"What brings you to Spring Forest?"

Aiden stared at something over Calum's shoulder. "Is there somewhere we can go and talk?"

Calum closed the door. "My office is always off-limits when the door is closed."

"If you don't mind, I'd like to go somewhere so we can eat."

In spite of himself, Calum was intrigued by the surprise visit and Aiden wanting to go somewhere to talk other than Calum's private office. "Okay. Just let me close out what I'm working on, and then we can head on over to the Grille." The Main Street Grille was his favorite go-to eating establishment for lunch and dinner when he wanted something more substantial than Pins and Pints had to offer.

He returned to the desk, tapped several keys and saved the data.

"I like your little town."

Smiling, Calum scooped a set of keys off the desk. "So do I." He opened the door and waited for Aiden to walk out of the office before closing and locking it.

"Much better than Raleigh?" Aiden asked.

"It has its advantages."

"What about disadvantages, Ramsey?"

Calum gave him a sidelong glance as they left the bowling alley. Dressed in a meticulously tailored cobalt-blue suit, Aiden looked like a walking *GQ* ad. He stood out in the more relaxed atmosphere of Spring Forest—a reminder of the fast-paced business world Calum had left behind.

"There aren't any. This is where I live and operate my business. Is there anything else you'd like to know?"

He knew he sounded defensive, but he resented Aiden's attempt to dis Spring Forest. The Hardings were to Raleigh banking and real estate what Bill Gates was to Microsoft. His friend had grown up in luxury. Calum wanted to remind Aiden that they came from different worlds and had different standards. They probably would've never crossed paths if he hadn't worked at the investment bank.

Aiden met Calum's eyes. "I didn't mean it to come out like that."

"Don't apologize, Harding. I'm just very protective of my hometown."

"That's what I want to talk to you about."

"Then, let's go eat. It gets pretty crowded at the Grille during lunchtime."

Calum hadn't taken more than three steps when he saw Lucy coming out of the bank. Slim-cut black jeans hugged her curves like a second skin. Her legs seemed go on forever in a pair of wedged sandals that added at least three inches to her statuesque figure. He was an even six foot and he estimated Lucy was only a few inches shorter. A black-and-white-striped headband held her hair off her face. She'd rolled up the cuffs of her white man-tailored shirt and in that instant he fantasized about her wearing his shirt and nothing underneath.

Lucy smiled and waved at him as she headed for Chapter One. Smiling, Calum returned her wave.

Get a grip, Ramsey, or you'll find yourself in too deep.

Fantasizing about getting Lucy Tucker into his bed was as dangerous as removing a pin from a hand grenade. Once out, it would take only seconds before detonating. And he'd likened Lucy's sexiness to a grenade and nitroglycerin—quiet and highly explosive.

He and Lucy were friends, and until and unless she indicated she wanted more than friendship, Calum would have to go along with their status. And even if she was ever interested in intimacy, she wasn't a woman with whom he could sleep without a commitment. Yes, he would be faithful to her because he believed in monogamy. But what if, after a while, she wanted more, and that more was marriage and children—two things he wasn't ready for at this time in his life?

"There's something I did notice about Spring Forest," Aiden said close to Calum's ear.

"What's that?"

"The women are stunning."

A wave of jealousy rendered Calum temporarily mute. He knew Aiden was referring to Lucy. "Are you thinking about having a bit of fun before you finally settle down with Jennifer?"

"Jen and I broke up last Christmas. The last time I ran into her sister a couple of months ago, she told me Jen was expecting a baby. I'll catch you up on what has been going on in my life after we eat. I've been existing on black coffee for days now and it's messing with my stomach."

Calum thought it odd that Aiden seemed so nonchalant about things ending with his long-time girlfriend. The two had met in college and were inseparable, the last he'd heard. Everyone on their team had teased Aiden relentlessly that he had to put a ring on the girl's finger or lose her; it was obvious that Jennifer had tired of waiting and had moved on.

Calum managed to find an empty booth along a side wall at the Main Street Grille and he and Aiden ordered burgers with a side of onion rings.

He waited for Aiden to finish his burger and half the onion rings, and then said, "Talk to me, friend."

"I guess it started with Jen. I knew she wanted to settle down—but even though I loved her, I just couldn't see that for myself. And after we split, I started thinking about other things in my life that weren't working for me. Including working for the investment firm. So I just walked out."

Calum leaned forward. "Walked out as in quitting?"

"Yes."

"What did your father say?"

Aiden concentrated on the food on his plate. "Some things I can't repeat." Shifting slightly on the burgundy-vinyl-covered booth seat, he gave Calum a long, penetrating stare. "It's taken me a while, but

I finally understand why you decided to give up the crazy-ass world of investing to work for yourself. Yes, we make a lot of money for other people, but at the expense of not having any time to enjoy it."

Calum nodded. There'd been times when he'd spent countless hours staring at the computer, watching the rise and fall of the market. But it hadn't ended there. At any hour of the night his cell phone would ring, or he would receive emails about clients on the other side of the world that needed his attention right away.

"Let me level with you, Harding. Right now, I'm putting in just as many hours as I did before. The upside is I'm working for myself. I'm not certain how long I'll be able to keep up that pace. Eventually, I'm going to need to hire an assistant manager."

"Have you advertised for one?"

"Not yet."

"Then don't."

A slight frown appeared between Calum's eyes. "What are you talking about?"

"If you need an assistant, then I'm your man."

Throwing back his head, Calum laughed, causing other diners to glance over at him. He sobered quickly. "All that caffeine must be messing with your stomach *and* your brain. You really want to move out here and work in a bowling alley?"

Aiden ran a hand over his face. "My father has been pressuring me to step up and take my rightful place at the company. This morning, I finally got the nerve to tell him I wanted no part of the Harding banking dynasty and left my letter of resignation on his desk."

Calum stared at Aiden as if he'd grown a third eye. He'd considered Aiden a pretty close friend back when they were working together, and at no time had Calum suspected Aiden was conflicted about working for his family-owned-and-operated investment bank.

"What I don't understand is why did you wait until now?" Calum questioned.

"You're asking me a question I really can't answer. I suppose it's like folks who continue to work at a job they hate for more than half their lives because they fear change. It's been that way for me since graduating college. Even when I'd interned at the bank in high school, I knew it wasn't where I wanted to work, but I didn't think I had a choice."

Calum wanted to tell Aiden he'd had advantages most young men and women craved after graduating high school or college: a position with a prominent company waiting for them without having to interview for it.

"I don't want to sound unsympathetic, Harding, but I'm not sure where I fit into your 'poor little rich boy' tale of woe."

"I want to invest in your company."

Shaking his head, Calum chuckled. "You're incredible. You claim you want to work for me then you flip the script and say you want to become an investor." His expression grew hard. "Not interested. The business is staying one hundred percent mine."

He'd sacrificed a social life while investing the proverbial blood, sweat and tears into Pins and Pints. No, he thought. He didn't want or need someone to carve out a slice of his business just because they had disposable resources.

Aiden managed to look sheepish. "I didn't mean to insult you."

"I'm not offended. I'm just not interested."

"Sorry about that."

"I want you to level with me, Harding. What do you really want?"

"I want what you have, Ramsey."

Calum frowned. "How do you know what I have?" They'd been friendly back in Raleigh, but they hadn't really kept in touch.

"I don't know everything, but you can't deny you are determining your own destiny. That's what I want, Calum. If investing in you is off the table, that's fine—but I'm serious about wanting that assistant manager position. What do you say?"

Calum sat motionlessly, mulling it all over. He knew it could not have been easy for Aiden to say all that. He'd never been one to talk about his problems and he'd never even hinted that he hadn't liked working for his family's bank. However, away from the office, he had tended to overindulge. Looking back, Calum wondered if Aiden's partying had been to release the buildup of frustration with his life.

"Let me think about it," he said after a lengthy pause. It wasn't as if he didn't need an assistant manager—and Calum was familiar with Aiden's ability to put people at ease and to quickly resolve interpersonal issues. "But, if I decide to bring you on board, I want to warn you that it's not a nine-to-five position. Pins and Pints is open eleven to eleven Monday through Thursday, and eleven to one o'clock Friday and Saturday, noon to eleven on Sunday. We'll work out a schedule, but you'll have to give up your duplex because I doubt you'll want to drive twenty miles back to Raleigh after closing up at one in the morning."

Aiden nodded. "That's not a problem. Knowing Dad, he's probably packing up my stuff as we speak. Even if you don't hire me, I don't plan to stay in Raleigh."

"I never said I *would* hire you, Harding. I said I would have to think about it."

A hint of a smile tilted the corners of Aiden's mouth. "Okay. By the way, do you know of any rentals or properties for sale around here?"

"Harris Vega is our local house flipper. He just may have a few available rentals."

Aiden pulled out his cell phone and entered the name Calum gave him. "I'll definitely look him up."

"As soon as I get back to the office and finish payroll, I'll work up a schedule where I think I could best use you," Calum said. "And if you agree, then we can talk salary."

Aiden slowly shook his head. "This is not about money."

Calum smiled. "You think I don't know that?" Aiden had been born into wealth, so for him money was not an issue. Rising slightly, Calum removed a money clip from the front pocket of his jeans and signaled for the waitress to bring the check. "I have to get back now."

Aiden placed his hand over Calum's. "I've got this. I'm going to order dessert, so why don't you go back to work? Besides, I've taken up enough of your time."

Calum put the money clip away. "It's been time well spent."

"I know for me it has," Aiden admitted. "I think I'm going to hang out in Spring Forest for a while to take in the sights before heading back to Raleigh and into the belly of the beast."

Calum rested a comforting hand on Aiden's shoulder. "Good luck with that." He stood. "I'll call you in a couple of days."

He didn't want to tell the man that he had already made up his mind to hire him, and that his decision wasn't completely altruistic. With an assistant, he would have more time for himself—and maybe for other relationships. He left the Grille and walked past Chapter One, thinking of the woman he'd like to devote some time to…if they could find a way to make it work.

Chapter Three

It took Calum less than thirty-six hours to plan a new shift schedule with Aiden Harding as the assistant manager. When he'd called Aiden to give him the news he was hiring him, there'd been silence for a full thirty seconds before Aiden thanked him and asked that he give him a couple of days to finalize his move to Spring Forest.

Calum called an impromptu meeting with his team of employees to inform them he'd hired an assistant manager. Whispers followed his announcement, and he knew his workers were apprehensive about who they would have to answer to in his absence.

It had taken Calum several weeks to interview and finally hire a staff he could trust and depend on to keep Pins and Pints running smoothly. He hoped they knew he would still look after them, even if he wasn't always the manager on-site.

After the meeting, Calum let the head bartender, Jake, know that he was going to be out for an hour, and he would be forwarding all calls to him. Jake had, understandably, looked shocked. Calum was always reachable by phone. He had two cell phones, one for the bowling alley and the other for his personal use. There was also a landline in the office as a backup if cell service was spotty or failed during violent thunderstorms or a tornado, like the one that had touched down damaging properties and nearly destroying Furever Paws the year before. But just now, just for the next hour, Calum wanted to be left undisturbed.

He headed for Chapter One. When he'd read the flyer announcing the Teddy Bear Storytime, he'd been curious to see what Lucy had planned for the young attendees.

As he entered the bookstore, he realized he wasn't the only one interested. A small group of adults milled around the bookstore as Lucy's Thursday assistant set out folding chairs. He smiled when he noticed more than a half dozen young children wearing pajamas and clutching stuffed animals sitting on beanbag cushions. One toddler rubbed her eyes, while another stuck his thumb in his mouth and cradled his tattered floppy-eared rabbit to his chest.

Calum couldn't pull his gaze off Lucy as she

folded her body down to a low stool in front of the children that were suddenly alert as she held up a book for them to see the cover. He knew she'd been an elementary school teacher in Charlotte, and there were occasions when he'd wanted to ask her why she'd left teaching to open a bookstore. Spring Forest was a small town with very few secrets about its residents, yet Lucy managed to remain an enigma to many. However, whenever he attempted to get her to talk about her past, she shut down. After a while, he'd respected her right to privacy and never broached the subject again.

He refused Miss Grace's offer to sit, preferring to stand near the door and watch Lucy.

Within seconds of Lucy opening *Brown Bear, Brown Bear, What Do You See?* the children were enraptured. Calum found himself totally engrossed in the dulcet sound of her voice. It was soft, comforting, rising and falling with enough animation that pulled listeners in, not letting them go until the book ended. Everyone applauded, including the adults.

"Read another one!" yelled a little girl with dark curls.

A redheaded boy jumped up. "No! I want the brown bear again!"

Lucy held up a hand and the debate between the children ended abruptly. "Every time you come, I will read different books. If you want to hear a certain story again, then your mommy or daddy can read it to you." She glanced over at the parents. "Extra copies of the books I'm reading tonight are on the table up front."

Smiling, Calum crossed his arms over his chest. He had to give it to Lucy. She'd known what it would take to raise interest and sell books. And this time it was children's books. During February, it had been romance for Valentine's Day, and titles geared to Black writers for Black History Month. She read three more books: *Chicka Chicka Boom Boom*, *The Very Hungry Caterpillar* and the classic *Goodnight Moon*.

The session ended with children telling their parents which books they wanted to take home. Lucy and her assistant were busy ringing up the purchases and packing the books in recyclable bags with teddy bear logos.

Lucy noticed Calum lingering after everyone left. Although she knew he was currently single, she didn't know whether he'd ever been married or had children. "Did you come to purchase books for your kids?"

He stroked his goatee with a forefinger. "I don't have any children. But I would like you to recommend a book for my four-year-old niece and nephew."

"So, you're an uncle?"

He flashed a wide grin. "An uncle of twins."

"You sound like a very proud uncle."

His eyebrows lifted. "That's me. They're very special."

Lucy met his light brown eyes and struggled to remain in control of her emotions. The more she saw Calum, the more she was forced to acknowledge that she liked him—liked him the way a woman liked a man.

She'd convinced herself since fleeing from Charlotte that she didn't want or need a man in her life, but just the mere presence of Calum Ramsey kept telling her that she was lying to herself. As a single woman in her twenties, she should've been dating and going to happy hours after work instead of driving home and having a one-sided conversation with her foster dog.

Lucy lowered her eyes, fearing he would see the yearning lurking in their depths. "Are they readers?"

"Yes. My sister is a teacher, and the house is filled with books."

"I can select a few that may appeal to them. But if they already have them, just bring them back and I'll exchange them."

"Show me what you recommend, and I'll text my sister to find out if she has them."

Lucy walked to the children's section and found two titles she knew were popular with children aged three to seven. When she returned to the front of the store, she found him folding the chairs and storing them on the dolly.

"You don't have to do that."

"That's okay. I just thought I'd give you a hand before you lock up."

"Do you realize how often you give me a hand, Calum?"

"No, I don't," he said, placing the last chair on the dolly.

"A lot. I don't know if I'll ever be able to repay you."

"I can think of one way," he said in a quiet voice.

"What's that?" Her heart was beating so loud, she wondered if Calum could hear it through her chest.

"Have dinner with me."

Lucy swallowed a nervous laugh. Did he mean dinner or...*dinner*? And which did she want him to mean? Her mind was giving one answer and her body a different one.

"When?"

"Sunday after next. At my place."

If they were going to have their first date then Lucy wanted it to be on her terms. "Okay, but only if it's at my place." She handed him the books.

When Calum asked Lucy to dinner, he hadn't expected her to agree, and he definitely hadn't expected her to invite him to her home. He'd been to her house once before, when she'd brought Buttercup home from Furever Paws. He'd carried Buttercup to the front door, but hadn't gone inside.

"Okay. Your house." He paused, his gaze fixed on her sexy mouth. "Are you cooking?"

She narrowed her eyes. "I'm not completely help-less in the kitchen."

"I didn't mean it like that," Calum said quickly, fearing he'd insulted her. That was the last thing he'd wanted to do.

"What exactly did you mean, Calum?"

He hesitated and knew he had to choose his words carefully. "If you didn't feel like cooking, I could always order something from Veniero's." The town's newest restaurant featured fine dining in the form of authentic southern Italian cuisine.

"You want Italian food?"

"I like Italian food."

She smiled. "Then Italian it is. Do you have any food allergies?"

"Nope. What do you plan to make?"

"I don't know. But I have more than a week to come up with something."

Calum had told her the following Sunday because he would arrange for Aiden to cover for him. "Do you want me to bring anything?"

"No thank you."

"How about wine?"

Lucy shook her head. "No wine. I have a few bottles in the house, but I rarely drink it. Any kind of alcohol puts me straight to sleep."

"Are you saying you're a cheap date?" Calum teased, smiling.

She scrunched up her nose. "Very cheap."

"We have something in common because I rarely touch alcohol."

"Are you in recovery?"

"No," he answered truthfully, but didn't elaborate further. He *did* have some negative history with alcohol abuse, but the alcoholic in question wasn't him—it was his father. And the absolute last thing Calum wanted was to follow in the man's footsteps.

"Then you wouldn't mind if I serve mocktails."

"Not at all."

"Do you know what I find odd, Calum?" Lucy questioned.

"What is that?"

"You run a business with 'pints' in its name and yet you don't drink."

He smiled and angled his head. "When I had to come up with a name for the bowling alley, I thought Pins and Pints was appropriate. Besides, I like the alliteration."

Lucy nodded. "It does have a nice flow."

"Chapter One is perfect for a bookstore. In fact, most of the names for businesses in Spring Forest are descriptive. Barkyard Boarding and Furever Paws are all about pets, and Rethread for second-hand clothes While Pins and Pints offers bowling and beer."

Lucy had made it a practice to patronize most businesses in town. The exception was the bowling alley, which she'd only been to once or twice, and even then only to sample the food in the restaurant section. She hadn't bowled since the fourth grade when she'd been invited to a bowling birthday party, and made a mental note to visit Pins and Pints again soon. After all, Calum was her friend. She should support him, too.

She pointed to the books. "Let me know if these titles are okay?"

Calum took out his cell phone and sent a text to his sister. He didn't have to wait long for a response. "They don't have these. I'll take them. How much do I owe you?"

She shook her head at him as she rang up the books. "Nothing, Calum."

He shook his head. "No, Lucy. I can't let you give away your stock."

She took the books from him, and walked over to the front desk. "I'm not giving them away. Tell them they are gifts from their uncle's friend."

"Just this one time, Lucy."

"One time what?"

"I'll accept them as gifts tonight, but not in the future."

"Yada, yada, yada," she drawled.

Calum knew Lucy was brushing him off, and then decided it wasn't worth debating the issue. He'd gotten her to agree to dinner—better to quit while he was ahead.

Lucy returned and handed him a bag with the books. "I hope your niece and nephew enjoy the books."

"I'm certain they will. And I don't have to tell you that your Teddy Bear Storytime was a rousing success."

"We did get to sell quite a few children's books." Leaning in close, Lucy brushed a light kiss on his jaw. "Good night, Calum. I have to lock up and take Buttercup for a walk."

He went completely still. The light touch of Lucy's lips reminded Calum of when he was a boy and he would lie on the grass to watch for the emergence of fireflies. Some would come close enough to touch his face with their tiny wings. It had always felt magical to him—and so did the soft brush of Lucy's lips.

To play off the effect she had on him, he fumbled for something else to say. "Where is Buttercup?"

"I took her home. I wasn't certain how she would react with so many kids in the store."

He could tell that Lucy wanted to go home, too, but he wasn't ready to let her leave. Even though everything about her was imprinted on his brain like a permanent tattoo, the memory of her wasn't enough to satisfy him. He wanted to spend not minutes or hours, but uninterrupted days with her. And he hoped sharing a Sunday dinner together would be the beginning of so much more. Right now, Calum wasn't certain what that more was.

Did he want to sleep with her?

Yes, he did.

But only if that was what she wanted. After all, they had time, and neither was going anywhere.

"Do you want me to put the dolly away?"

"No. The rental company will come tomorrow and pick it up."

"You don't have to rent chairs, Lucy. I have dozens of tables and chairs in my stockroom. I'll make certain to bring them over next Thursday."

"You don't have to do…"

Covering Lucy's mouth with his, Calum stopped her protest. The kiss was meant to silence her, but it became more when he deepened the kiss as her lips parted under his.

What the hell are you doing?

Within seconds, Calum realized he'd made a serious faux pas. He was standing in the front of Chapter One, kissing the owner, where anyone passing by could witness their PDA.

He pulled back, holding the bag with the books in a death grip. "Do I need to apologize for that?" he asked softly. As wonderful as it had been, he hated the idea that he might have upset her. He breathed out in relief when she shook her head, looking dazed but not angry. "Good night, then, Lucy."

Turning on his heel, he opened the door and

walked out, even though he secretly ached to stay. Unknowingly, Lucy Tucker had woven an invisible spell over him from which he did not want to escape. And he was dying for a chance to uncover what made her so very different from the other women he'd known.

One thing he did know. She was the type of woman that made a man want to settle down and marry. She represented stability. And watching her interaction with the preschoolers told him she would be a wonderful mother.

Wife.

Mother.

Those were two words he refused to consider in connection to his life. He liked being single and unencumbered.

Calum returned to Pins and Pints, walked over to the bar and sat on a stool at the far end. The bartender came over and set a cocktail napkin on the polished surface.

"What are you having, boss?"

He stared at the man who was a throwback to the days of hippies and free love. Jake Reynolds had a long, gray, waist-length ponytail and wore multiple strands of colorful beads around his neck. He even owned a restored Volkswagen Karmann Ghia. Calum had gone through several bartenders until Jake had walked through the doors boasting there wasn't a drink he couldn't make. And it wasn't just bravado.

Calum had not only hired the mixologist but promoted him to supervise the other barkeeps.

"I'll have a beer." Calum watched Jake open a bottle of nonalcoholic beer, fill a pilsner glass, level off the foam and then set it on the napkin. "Thanks."

"Do you want me to call the kitchen and order something to go along with your brew?"

"No, thanks."

Resting his elbows on the bar, Jake leaned closer. "You need to do something to get her out of your system," he whispered.

Calum sat straight. "What are you talking about?"

A pair of dark gray eyes met his. "The cute little thing in the bookstore." Jake held up a large beefy hand. "Everyone knows you have a thing for her, Calum. Folks are talking about how much time you spend there, and it's not because you're buying books."

Calum stared at the bag on the stool next to his. He wanted to tell Jake to mind his own damn business but didn't want to appear defensive. After all, he was an adult and so was Lucy. They didn't have to hide like teenagers that were forbidden to see each other.

"Well, if folks are talking, then I should really give them something to talk about if I take her to Veniero's." He smiled when Jake gave him a fist bump.

"That's what I'm talking about, boss."

Calum took a sip of the chilled beer then remembered to take his phone off Do Not Disturb when the one at the bar rang. "I'll get it, Jake."

He answered the call from a woman who wanted to host a bowling birthday party for her eight-year-old daughter the last week in the month. Calum jotted her name and number on the napkin and told her he would call her back as soon as he checked the events calendar.

Picking up his beer, he headed for his office, unlocked the door and pulled up the month of May on the computer. As he focused on work, he put his thoughts about Lucy to the side...for now.

Lucy chided herself over and over for not stopping Calum's kiss. Not only had she kissed him back, but she had parted her lips to allow his tongue inside her mouth.

It had taken hours for her to fall asleep and by the time she finally had, it was time for her to get up. When she'd stared at her reflection in the mirror over the bathroom vanity, she groaned aloud. The slight puffiness under her eyes was evidence of a restless night and it was the first time in a long time that she had to use concealer.

She fed and walked Buttercup before assisting her into the cargo area of the Toyota RAV4. The SUV was a college graduation gift from her father, and had come as a complete surprise for Lucy. She and her father rarely spoke to each other.

Adam Tucker had divorced her mother the year Lucy'd celebrated her tenth birthday. After that, their interactions were mostly financial, with him sending her mother child support payments every month and paying her college tuition. Lucy was shocked once her engagement was announced that he'd offered to give her away. It had taken a lot of soul-searching for her to agree, not wanting to hurt her mother. But then, when Lucy was twenty-one, her mother eventually moved on with her life when she married a widower with three adult children, while Adam hadn't remarried.

Lucy parked in the parking lot behind the row of stores and unlocked the rear door to Chapter One. She'd arrived two hours early because the party rental company was scheduled to come and pick up the chairs at eight.

Buttercup moved slowly as she made her way over to her bed. She lay down and Lucy noticed a lot of movement in the dog's abdomen. It was growing very close to the time when Buttercup would deliver her litter. She'd already set up a nesting location at home. This was her first experience with a pregnant dog and she was both nervous and excited. She'd given her assistants keys to open the bookstore in case Buttercup whelped her pups during the day.

A man from the party rental company retrieved the dolly with the chairs, and at exactly ten she turned on the lights, reversed the sign and unlocked the door. Morning hours were slow with maybe one or two customers. There was usually a steady flow of people coming into the bookstore to browse or make purchases in the afternoon to just before closing at six.

The bell chimed minutes after Miss Grace walked in and a young man entered with a shopping bag. "Mr. Ramsey wanted me to give this to you."

"Wait!" Lucy called out, but he was in and out of the store in under a minute.

She peered into the bag and removed containers with a garden salad, tempura, chicken fingers and a cup of pea soup. Lucy smiled and shook her head. She was on to Calum. Because she wouldn't let him pay for the books, he'd decided to repay her with food. And he knew she took her lunch hour at one when her assistants arrived for their shift.

Reaching into the pocket of her smock, she took out her cell phone and tapped his number.

"Pins and Pints."

"May I please speak to Calum Ramsey?"

"Who's calling?"

"Lucy Tucker from Chapter One bookstore."

"Miss Tucker, Calum is on a call with a vendor."

"Can you please let him know I called, and I'd like him to call me back? He has my number."

"I'll definitely let him know you called."

"Thank you." Although she'd brought her lunch, Lucy wasn't about to let what Calum sent her go to waste.

"Something smells good," Miss Grace remarked.

Lucy smiled at the petite woman with bluish-gray permed hair. "It's from Pins and Pints."

"My doctor has put me on a strict diet after my last physical, so I have to watch my salt intake and avoid fried foods, so eating at the bowling alley is a no-no for me. When I was your age, I could eat anything, but now I have a list of dos and don'ts, and that drives me crazy." She waved her hand. "Go and enjoy your lunch. I'll take care of the front."

Lucy walked to the back and closed the door. Buttercup was still sleeping, and she decided not to wake her up to feed her. She washed her hands and then sat down to eat. She was glad there was no one to witness her moan with pleasure as she ate. Everything was beyond delicious. It was the best split-pea soup she'd ever eaten and the subtle heat from the chicken fingers lingered on her palate, triggering a thirst she offset with a bottle of chilled water.

Buttercup was up after Lucy finished her lunch and she fed the dog. A half hour later, Buttercup barked to let her know she wanted to go out.

The afternoon passed and Calum didn't return her call. Lucy wondered if he hadn't gotten her message or he had no intention of calling her back. She didn't want to fight with him about the cost of two books, so she decided there was another way to get back at him.

It was Friday—the beginning of the weekend— and it was time she showed up at Pins and Pints to hang out for a few hours. It had been a while since she'd gone to a happy hour.

"Buckle up, Mr. Ramsey," she whispered as she drove home. "It's about to get a little wild and bumpy."

Chapter Four

When Lucy arrived at Pins and Pints to find a crowd lining up behind the food truck selling tacos outside the bowling alley, she felt like she'd stepped back in time.

She used to go to happy hours with coworkers in Charlotte. She went along not to drink but to enjoy a camaraderie with her fellow teachers. But then she'd found out the camaraderie had an edge. One of the teachers in their social circle was a snitch who would openly agree with some of the complaints about one of their assistant principals, then go back and tell her who'd said what.

The experience had soured Lucy on those happy hour outings, making her stick closer to the people she'd thought she could trust—like her best friend and boyfriend. Of course, they hadn't proved trustworthy, either.

For a second, she thought about just going home, giving up the plan for a night out. But like the name of her bookstore, Lucy was beginning chapter one of her best new life. It was Friday night, and she was going to put herself out there for once—at least for a few hours. Then she'd return home to check on Buttercup.

When she entered the bowling alley, Lucy was met with a cacophony of sounds from balls striking pins, cheers and groans from bowlers, laughter from those sitting at tables and the bar, and the driving, pumping rhythm of a classic Rihanna club tune spun by a DJ. The joint was truly jumping.

She felt someone tap her shoulder and she turned around to find Calum with a stunned look on his face. He'd exchanged his ubiquitous tee and jeans for a black untucked shirt, matching slacks and shiny low-heeled boots.

"Since it's been a while since my last visit, I decided to come and see for myself what makes Pins and Pints the go-to place on weekends."

Calum had not believed his eyes when Lucy had walked in. At first, he hadn't recognized her, but it was her sexy walk that had given her away. Her wavy hair was a profusion of tiny curls moving as if taking on a life of their own. However, it was her face and dress that had rendered him unable to move or speak for several seconds. Smoky eye makeup, crimson lipstick and the little black dress that revealed an extravagant amount of bare skin had him ogling her like a lovestruck adolescent.

Calum had to remind himself that he wasn't sixteen years old but thirty, and he should've been much more secure when interacting with a woman he found himself attracted to. And he liked Lucy, whether bare-faced and wearing a smock that hid her curves or with makeup and a body-hugging, off-the-shoulder dress ending well above her knees. He took a surreptitious glance at her long, shapely bare legs and the black stilettos that brought her up to his height.

"What's the matter, Calum?" Lucy whispered in his ear. "Cat got your tongue?"

He cupped her elbow and steered her in the direction of the bar. "Do you like what you've come to see?"

Smiling, she nodded. "Yes."

Calum seated Lucy on the stool next to his reserved one. Everyone that came into Pins and Pints knew that the two stools at the far end of the bar were for the owner. He leaned closer, his mouth mere inches from her ear with a tiny diamond hoop. "And I happen to like what I see."

Lucy turned her head. "Mr. Ramsey, are you flirting with me?"

"Yes, I am, Miss Tucker. Does that bother you?"

A mysterious smile parted her lips. "No. In fact, I like it."

Calum also smiled. "Now that we're on the same page, I think it's time we begin chapter two." Throwing back her head and baring her throat, Lucy laughed, bringing his gaze to linger on her long neck. A neck he wanted to taste before moving lower. Each time she took a breath, he couldn't pull his gaze away from the swell of breasts rising above the revealing décolletage. She looked and smelled incredible. If she had come to the bowling alley to make a statement—then he was hearing it loud and clear. She had turned him all the way up *and* on.

He signaled for Jake. "Give the lady whatever she wants and put it on my tab."

Lucy smiled at the bartender. "I'll have a virgin margarita."

"And I'll have sparkling water with lime," Calum said. His right arm went around her waist. "Can Jake order something from the kitchen for you?" Lucy lowered her eyes and glanced up at him through her lashes, looking incredibly sensual.

"No, thank you. Speaking of food, I want to thank you for sending over lunch."

"I did get your message to return your call, but I got tied up with other matters. I'm sorry about that—

I never want you to think that I'm blowing you off. By the way, next week I'm going to be unavailable because I'll be involved with training my new assistant manager."

Lucy chided herself for thinking he'd blown her off. As a business owner she knew personal feelings were secondary to taking care of whatever the business needed. And she knew if she was going to have an open and honest relationship with Calum, then she wanted to trust him and for him to trust her.

"I need to tell you something."

"What's that?"

"I thought you didn't call me back because you knew I was going to tell you that there was no need to bring me lunch. Especially if you were only doing it because I refused payment for your niece and nephew's books."

"I'm not one to engage in tit for tat, Lucy. I sent you lunch because I thought you'd enjoy it. There's nothing wrong with treating yourself. You have assistants that can cover for you, so you should get out and eat at the Grille a couple of times a week."

Lucy stared at his strong masculine mouth, remembering how it felt and tasted when he'd kissed her. Calum's kissing was a reminder of what she'd been missing for far too long. What she'd been denying even longer. She knew he was right—she did deserve to treat herself sometimes to things just because they felt good. And she felt sure that being with him would be so, so good. She was still uncertain about whether she was ready for a relationship, but she knew she wanted to be with him.

"Once Buttercup and her puppies are adopted, you can let me know when you want to share lunch at the Grille."

Calum's arm tightened around her waist as he leaned closer to kiss her hair. "That's a deal."

The bartender set their cocktails on the bar. Lucy lifted the chilled glass with the pale green liquid and touched it to Calum's highball glass. "The only way to have a friend is to be one." When he gave her a questioning look, she explained. "That's a quote from Ralph Waldo Emerson."

"Is that how you think of us, Lucy?"

"Yes. We are friends until..." Her words trailed off.

His eyebrows lifted. "Until what?"

She set the glass down to conceal the tremors racing up and down her arm. Lucy felt as if everything around her had disappeared, leaving her and Calum as the only two in the cavernous space filled with throngs of patrons bowling, eating and drinking. She knew she had his full, undivided attention as he waited to hear what she'd say.

"Until circumstances change us."

Calum touched her glass. "I'll drink to that."

"What are you drinking to?" asked a man standing less than a foot away.

* * *

Calum swiveled on his stool to find Aiden grinning at him like a Cheshire cat, cursing the man's timing. He stood. "I wasn't expecting you until next week."

"I'm renting one of Harris Vega's houses in Kingdom Creek. I had my stuff from Raleigh delivered this afternoon. It's going to take a while for me to unpack, but I'm ready to start working whenever you are."

Although Aiden was talking to him, Calum noticed that he couldn't take his eyes off Lucy. He shifted, resting a proprietary hand at the small of her back. "Lucy, this is Aiden Harding, my new assistant manager. Aiden, Lucy Tucker. She's the owner of the Chapter One bookstore."

Lucy reached over, extending her hand. "It's nice meeting you, Aiden."

Aiden took her hand and kissed her fingers. "It's *my* pleasure, Lucy. It looks as if I'll be doing a lot more reading now that I live here."

Jealousy shot through Calum like lightning across a nighttime sky. It had taken time and patience for Calum to convince Lucy that they could be business neighbors *and* friends. Where did Aiden get off flirting with her on the first meeting?

He felt her body go stiff, and then his arm circled her waist again.

A slight frown flitted across Lucy's features. "May I please have my hand back?"

That's my girl, he thought. It was obvious she hadn't succumbed to Aiden's practiced charm.

Aiden released her hand, smiling. "Sorry about that."

"That's okay." Lucy lifted her chin, smiling. "Calum, darling, I think I need something to eat because this drink is really strong."

He bit his lip to keep from laughing. She was quite the actress, putting on such a show to make it clear she was there with Calum—and lying through her pretty teeth, given that her cocktail was nonalcoholic. "It's okay, bae. I'll have Jake call the kitchen and tell them to bring you something." He assisted her off the stool. "You can wait at my table."

Calum led her to a small table for two and removed the Reserved sign. He seated Lucy and then leaned down to kiss her. "What do you want to eat?"

"Surprise me." Reaching up, Lucy rested a hand on his shoulder. "Thank you, darling."

He leaned in to kiss her temple and whispered in her ear, "You are as consummate an actress as you are beautiful."

Lucy demurely lowered her eyes, and Calum wanted them to be anywhere but in the crowded bowling alley. She triggered something he'd never experienced with any other woman. Of all the women he'd been with, Calum knew Lucy Tucker was the only one who would be forever indelible.

"You talk a lot of trash, Calum."

He winked at her. "I don't think so."

Calum walked over to the bar to have Jake place an order with the kitchen. He had to get away from Lucy because he feared spooking her by admitting that what he felt and had been feeling for her surpassed friendship. And it wasn't just about sex. It was about the elusive calmness he'd spent most of his life chasing. His mother had called him her restless child because he hadn't known what he'd wanted to be. He'd flitted from one interest to another, hoping to find his niche. It had taken years before he'd realized he needed to work for himself and at his own pace.

He'd felt happier and more fulfilled once he'd opened Pins and Pints, but true peace had still eluded him…until Lucy Tucker came along.

Aiden was leaning with his back to the bar when Calum stood next to him. "Is there something you need to tell me so I can take my foot out of my mouth?"

"What are you talking about?"

"Lucy Tucker."

"What about her, Aiden?"

"Is she taken?"

A shiver of annoyance snaked up Calum's spine. He'd hired Aiden to pick up some of the slack and free up his schedule. The man hadn't even begun working and his concern was about coming on to a woman. That rubbed Calum the wrong way. Especially if that woman was someone Calum coveted for himself.

"That's something you'll have to ask her, Aiden, because I don't speak for Lucy."

Aiden nodded. "Consider the subject moot."

Not only was it moot, but it was off the table for future discussion. Calum half listened to Aiden as he watched one of the volunteers at Furever Paws approach Lucy and sit beside her. There was too much chatter for him to overhear what was being said as Lucy nodded. Then he was distracted when cheering erupted from the patrons at the bar. The basketball season was winding down and teams were vying with one another to make the playoffs.

Calum wanted to sit with Lucy but knew that was impossible because he was working. He shifted his attention to Aiden. "If you want, I can show you around or you can just hang out and observe."

"I think I'm going to hang out."

"I'm going to schedule two staff meetings on Tuesday to introduce you to the day and then night shifts."

"What about Monday?" Aiden questioned.

"That'll be orientation. I will give you a step-by-step tutorial of what it takes to operate a bowling alley." Calum rested a hand on the sleeve of Aiden's tailored silk and linen jacket. "By the way, your wardrobe will have to go. Jeans, boots, tees and tennis shoes are the day-to-day norm. We get a little fancy on Friday because couples come here after work, and Saturday is date night, but even then, a full suit and tie is too much."

Aiden pointed to Calum's untucked shirt. "That's fancy?"

"Don't knock my threads, Mr. *GQ*. You'll find out soon enough that Spring Forest is not a super-fancy town."

Calum assumed it would take time for Aiden to shed his big-city mindset before becoming acclimated to living and working in a small town. But he believed the man was up to the challenge. During his tenure at Harding Investments, he'd admired Aiden's managerial competence. It made for quite a contrast with the way he'd revert to a frat boy whenever he held social events at his duplex.

Calum was certain he and Aiden would work well together, otherwise he never would've committed to hiring him.

"Ramsey?"

"Yes, Harding."

"I have a confession to make."

Calum gave Aiden a sidelong glance. "Talk to me."

"I now see why you left Raleigh. This place has a nice vibe."

"Is it too calm for you?"

Aiden ran a hand over his face. "No. I need some tranquility in life. Breaking up with Jen made me realize I can have a good time without turning my place into a club. For now, I just want to relax and enjoy myself."

"Are you saying you're not looking for a relationship?"

"That's exactly what I'm saying."

"Well, your personal life isn't really any of my business. In general, I try to leave people to do their own thing, as long as they get the job done. However, I do have one stringent rule everyone must follow or risk termination."

"What's that?"

"You're not permitted to drink alcohol during your shift."

"Did something happen for you to institute that rule?" Aiden asked.

Calum nodded. "I had a guy assigned to shoe rental who had too many one night and got into an argument with a customer. It would've escalated into a physical confrontation if I hadn't intervened."

"Did you fire him?"

"Not initially. I discovered he had a drinking problem and gave him an ultimatum. Go into treatment or lose your job. He refused to acknowledge he had a problem, so I had no alternative but to let him go." Alcoholism was too touchy a topic for him to be able to just let it slide—not that he'd get into that with Aiden.

His attention shifted when one of the kitchen servers said the cook needed to see him. He went to see what the talented man wanted; fifteen minutes later he returned to the bar and looked for Lucy.

He schooled his expression not to reveal his disappointment when Jake told him she'd left.

Calum's discontent was short-lived, knowing he would spend more than a few minutes with her the following Sunday. And with tonight, he felt like something between them had shifted. She'd shown up, all dressed up, and seemed open to him in a way she never had been before. It made him hopeful that their friendship might be moving forward into something new.

He couldn't *wait* for Sunday.

Lucy repositioned the water glasses and then took a step back to observe the place settings on the dining room table. She was eight when her mother had taught her how to set a table for formal and informal dining. When she'd questioned why she had to know the differences between a red wineglass and a water goblet, Myra Tucker told her how her mother-in-law had openly chastised her for using the wrong glass for water. Lucy never forgot her mother's pained expression when divulging the story. After that, she threw all her energies into memorizing where every item should be positioned on the table.

As she'd matured, Lucy's strained relationship with her paternal grandmother had been the opposite of the one she had with her maternal grandmother.

Her father's mother was haughty, critical and snobbish, while Lucinda Taylor was affectionate, nurturing and kind. They'd both left their mark on her in different ways—but with her maternal grandmother, she was actually grateful for the memories. Grammie was gone, yet there were still blessed times when Lucy felt her presence. It always brought her comfort.

Buttercup walked into the dining area and pressed her nose against Lucy's ankle. "I need you to be on your best behavior," Lucy explained, "because Calum is coming over. I don't want you to embarrass me when you start growling or barking."

A few days ago, Lucy had noticed a change in the dog's behavior whenever she walked her. Normally calm and friendly, she'd growl and bark, prompting people to keep their distance. She even barked at Lucy's assistants whenever they ventured into the back office. Lucy wondered if Buttercup would return to her sunny disposition after becoming a mother or remain standoffish and overly protective of her pups.

She scratched Buttercup behind her ears. "I'm going to take a shower now, and then I need to get dressed before Calum gets here." Buttercup nudged her leg again. "I'll be right back, sweetie."

Lucy still did not understand how the dog had become so attached to her—and vice versa—in such a short period of time. It was as if they'd bonded instantly when their eyes had met at Furever Paws Animal Rescue.

She headed for her bedroom and the en suite bath, one of her favorite parts of the house. Lucy had instantly fallen in love with the small three-bedroom house that had been so beautifully remodeled. Harris Vega had gutted the one-story structure and removed walls to create an open-floor-plan concept. New stainless-steel kitchen appliances and refinished hardwood floors topped her list of must-haves. She also loved the half-bath with a shower off the kitchen, the spacious pantry, the laundry room and the fenced-in backyard.

The lease she'd signed was coming due in four months and she had to decide whether to renew the lease or consider purchasing the house. She was seriously considering buying. The only drawback was the size of the rooms. The master bedroom was smaller than the one in her Charlotte condo, and she could only fit a full-size bed, nightstand and chest of drawers in the guest bedroom. The third bedroom was even smaller.

Stripping off her clothes and leaving them in a hamper, she stepped into the free-standing shower stall. As she showered, she thought about all Calum had done for her in the past week. Although she hadn't seen him in person, he'd kept his promise to have chairs brought to the bookstore for her Thursday Teddy Bear Storytime. The young man who had delivered her lunch the first day had been pressed into service, arriving at exactly one o'clock every day with a shopping bag from which wafted mouth-watering aromas. The cook at Pins and Pints alternated soup and sandwich days with cobb, spinach and Greek salads.

Calum had mentioned an interest in Italian food for Sunday dinner. She was willing to comply, even though, for Lucy, Sunday dinners were quintessential Southern with either fried chicken or baked ham. Sides included collard or mustard greens, fried cabbage with bacon, candied sweet potatoes or potato salad. Cornbread was the norm but occasionally her grandmother would bake a pan of fluffy buttery biscuits. Lemon pound cake, bread pudding, pecan and sweet potato pies were her favorite desserts. That was what Sunday dinner meant to her…but for Calum, she was willing to try something different, to take a chance and see whether or not it worked out.

She had spent the week preparing for Sunday. She'd dedicated one night to doing laundry, another to cleaning the house and another to buying groceries.

Lucy did not want to think of inviting Calum to her home as a date but as an offer of appreciation for all his help. *The only way to have a friend is to be one.* The Emerson quote was one of her favorites and that's what Calum Ramsey had become to her. As a friend, he was something Johnny had never been and could never be. And maybe tonight, she'd find out if they could be something more.

Chapter Five

Calum got out of his car, carrying the house gifts for Lucy. He'd been raised to never go to someone's house empty-handed. Despite Lucy's insistence she didn't need anything, he'd decided to bring something he hoped she would appreciate. Buttercup appeared on the top step, tail wagging, and whining.

Lucy smiled. "It appears she's happy to see you."

"It has been a while since we've seen each other." Calum dipped his head and kissed Lucy's cheek. Her warmth and the familiar scent of her perfume reminded him of how much he'd missed her. "Sorry, I know I'm early."

"That's okay."

Lucy opened the door wider, and he wiped his

feet on a thick sisal mat and walked into her home
for the first time. Buttercup hovered at his feet and
he reached down to give her a pat. Calum had grown
attached to the dog the instant Lucy had chosen to
foster Buttercup. When news went out that Furever
Paws needed fosters, he'd known he couldn't volunteer because of the number of hours he spent at
Pins and Pints. However, by helping Lucy with vet
appointments, he got to feel like he was part of fostering Buttercup, too. He liked it.

When he looked up from the dog, he was able
to fully take in the home in front of him. The open
concept permitted him an unobstructed view of a
seating grouping with a sofa, love seat and a chair in
a pale-yellow hue with navy blue throw pillows. A
mahogany coffee table with a large crystal-faceted
bowl was filled with yellow and blue glass beads.
The colors were repeated in an area rug. His stared
at the dining room table set with silver-rimmed dinnerware, silver and crystal.

"Your home is beautiful."

Lucy smiled. "Thank you."

Calum handed her the flowers. "I didn't know
what type of flowers you liked, so I decided to get a
mixed bouquet." The salesperson had recommended
variegated colored roses, tulips and mums.

"They're gorgeous, Calum. They will make the
perfect centerpiece for the table."

He showed her the potted plant he'd held behind

his back. "I also got the plant because I know flowers don't last long."

Lucy put a hand over her mouth. "How did you know?" she asked as she set the bouquet on a side table near the entryway.

"Know what?"

"That I collect orchids." She took the plant from him. "Come with me and I'll show you."

Calum concentrated on the wavy hair on her nape rather than Lucy's rounded hips in a pair of black linen slacks she'd paired with a white sleeveless silk blouse. Black leather ballet flats gave him the advantage of height, unlike when she'd worn the stilettos to Pins and Pints. He'd tried to forget the image of her in the sexy black dress that wantonly displayed her toned body and long, shapely legs, and failed. He'd suspected she knew the transformation would shock him—and others, as well, given that he'd noticed several men gawking at her slack-jawed as she'd strutted into the bowling alley.

Lucy, the chameleon, went from shopkeeper with her ubiquitous smock concealing her body to transforming herself into a sensual visual feast. And now, with her tailored slacks and blouse, he found her beautiful and sensual, but also more approachable, which served to put him totally at ease.

He followed her across the living and dining area to a hallway that led to bedrooms. The doors were open and Calum gave them a cursory glance until

Lucy stopped in front of the bedroom at the end of the hall. She stepped aside and he walked into the space that had been set up like a study with a floral-patterned chaise and bookcases packed tightly with books. Then he saw them.

A long table spanning the width of one wall was covered with hand-painted clay pots of colorful mini moth orchids and succulents. Midafternoon sunlight pouring into the windows had turned the space into a magic garden with rays of orange and gold where Lucy probably spent time when relaxing. He studied the framed color and black-and-white photographs of Lucy with various family members lining a table facing the chaise, while the soft sounds of gurgling water in a portable fountain created a spa-like atmosphere.

"This is the perfect space to unwind at the end of the day," Calum stated, moving closer to Lucy, her warmth triggering a need he refused to acknowledge. He and Lucy would remain friends until she indicated she wanted more.

Lucy set the plant with the snow-white delicate flower on the table, and turned to stare up at him. "It is where I come and spend a few hours reading and relaxing before I turn in for the night."

"I need a space like this, because once I get home, it takes me a while to unwind."

Lucy rested a hand over his chest. "That's because you spend too many hours working."

Calum nodded, smiling. "You're right. Now that Aiden's on board, it's going to allow me more time to myself."

"How is he working out?"

"Quite well."

"How are your employees adjusting to having an über-wealthy manager telling them what to do?"

Calum's eyebrows lifted slightly. "You know about Aiden's family money?"

Lucy folded her arms under her breasts. "Come now, Calum. Most people in North Carolina are familiar with the Hardings."

"What do you know about him?"

"Just that he belongs to one of the wealthiest families in Raleigh. When his parents announced his engagement, it was all over the local news. When you introduced him to me as your assistant manager, I couldn't believe you'd hired the Prince of Raleigh."

"Is that why you dissed him, Lucy? Because of his wealth?"

She shook her head. "No. I don't care how much he's worth. He pissed me off because he tried coming on to me while he's engaged to another woman."

Calum heard the bitterness in Lucy's voice and wondered if she'd experienced something similar. "Aiden is no longer engaged, so he's free to flirt with any woman he chooses."

"Count me out as one of those women. I was not impressed."

"Are you saying you would never date Aiden?"

A beat passed before she said, "I've never been attracted to blond men." She paused, seemingly deep in thought. "I take that back. Brad Pitt would be the exception."

Calum chuckled. "Brad Pitt is too old for you."

"Brad Pitt will never be too old for any woman," Lucy said with a laugh then eyed him speculatively. "Have you ever been in love, Calum?"

"I'd believed I was," he said truthfully.

"What happened?"

A wry smile flitted over his mouth. "She wanted something I wasn't ready to give her."

"Marriage?"

Calum nodded. "Yes. We were in college, and I wanted to wait until I knew I could support her and a family. She said it was now or never, so we went our separate ways."

"Not rushing to get married sounds reasonable."

"Maybe to you, but not to her."

Lucy shook her head, as if shaking the idea off. "Enough talk about other people, Calum. What are you going to do with all that extra time now that you have an assistant manager?"

Calum winked at her. "Perhaps I will be able to convince my friend and fellow businessperson to play hooky where we can spend some quality time together."

"That can't happen until Buttercup and her pup-

pies are adopted. I'm seriously thinking about sched-
uling shorter summer hours so I can be home more
with her and the puppies. I'd like to close on both
Sundays and Mondays during the months of June,
July and August."

"Good for you." Since she was the only full-time
employee, Lucy could choose the days when she was
open for operation, while it hadn't been the same
for Pins and Pints. His business was a seven-day-a-
week operation with a payroll of more than a dozen
full- and part-time employees. A major change to
the schedule would impact too many people for him
to consider it.

"Thank you again for the flowers and the plant.
Now, it's time we eat."

"Can I help you with anything?"

"No, Calum. You're my guest, and I didn't invite
you here to work. Besides, I have everything under
control."

Lucy had prepared everything in advance. She'd
made dessert the night before and chilled it in the
fridge. She had also prepped the chicken piccata,
stuffed mushrooms, and asparagus with pecorino
Romano. Then as an afterthought, she'd made spa-
ghetti with garlic and oil.

She filled a vase with water and arranged the
flowers, set it on the table and retreated to the half-
bath to wash her hands. She was unaware Calum had

followed her until he stood beside her, reaching over to get to the sink, as well.

"What are you doing?"

"I'm washing my hands so I can help you."

"I told you I have—"

"Everything under control," he said, cutting her off. "I know, Lucy, but I get antsy sitting around doing nothing."

Going on tiptoe, she kissed his ear. "You have to learn how to relax."

Reaching around her, Calum pumped the soap dispenser and held his hands under the running water. "I think I'll need some lessons in that. Is it possible for me to stay after class so you can tutor me?"

Lucy bit her lip to keep from laughing. "You may need some remedial classes before I take you on." Reaching for a paper towel from a stack on the vanity, she handed it to Calum before taking one for herself.

"I don't think so," he whispered against her nape. His arms circled her waist. "I'm a quick learner."

The pit of Lucy's stomach churned at the same time her heart pounded against her ribs. Calum was too close, too male—and he felt too good. She felt drugged by his heat, his masculine scent. Her knees buckled and she would've fallen if he hadn't held her upright.

"Calum," she whispered, not recognizing her own voice.

"It's okay, bae. We're not going to do anything you don't want."

Lucy nodded like a bobblehead doll. Even though she still didn't feel completely sure of herself, she knew that being with him wasn't just what she wanted. It was what she needed.

She needed Calum to help her forget the pain and humiliation that had forced her to flee Charlotte for Spring Forest.

She needed him to scale the wall she'd erected to keep men out of her life and out of her bed. She couldn't tear it down herself—she needed help. *His* help. Within minutes of first introducing herself to Calum, she'd felt the spark, in spite of all her vows not to ever be vulnerable or gullible again. She'd thought she would be fine with just friendship…up until the night of the Teddy Bear Storytime when he'd kissed her and she'd kissed him back. For Lucy, the kiss represented freedom—freedom to love again and, more importantly, the freedom to trust.

Did she trust Calum?

Yes.

Was she falling in love with her friend?

Yes!

Lucy closed her eyes and rested her head on Calum's shoulder. The familiar scent of fresh laundry on his pale-blue shirt and his bodywash wafted to her nostrils. She wanted to tell Calum that when she'd rejected Aiden by flirting with him instead, it hadn't just been an act. When she'd called him "darling," she'd wanted him to be just that and more.

Whining, following by a loud bark shattered the spell as Lucy extricated herself from Calum's arms to find Buttercup standing feet away.

"It looks as if your fur baby doesn't like me cuddling with her mama."

Lucy walked out of the bathroom. "She's been barking at people lately whenever I walk her. I believe she doesn't want them to get too close to her."

"It's not her she wants them at a distance from, Lucy. It's you. She's become very protective of you."

"Maybe you're right." Lucy had spent a lot of time pouring her heart out since Buttercup had become her therapy dog, and just maybe her foster pet's protective instincts had surfaced in response to Lucy's bouts of sadness and vulnerability.

"It's okay," Calum crooned as Buttercup continued to growl. "I'm not going to hurt your mama."

Lucy took Calum's hand. "Buttercup has to get used to seeing us together, outside of going to the vet."

"Speaking of us together, I want you to call me when she goes into labor."

"That may be in the middle of the night or when you're working."

"It doesn't matter, Lucy. I want to be here to help you."

"Should I assume you have some experience with a dog giving birth?"

Calum smiled. "Yes. My sister had a cockapoo that escaped when she'd left the back door open. The next thing we knew, a stray dog had gotten into the yard and was mating with her. Kayla was all the way hysterical."

"How old was your sister?"

"Nine. She'd gotten Princess as a puppy for Christmas, and we were waiting for her to turn five months before having her spayed. Well, Princess had other ideas. She wanted a boyfriend and when one came along, they did the deed."

Laughing and shaking her head, Lucy removed sheets of parchment off a tray of mushrooms stuffed with spicy sausage, onion and garlic, and another with asparagus drizzled with olive oil, garlic powder and pecorino Romano cheese. She glanced over at Calum perched on a stool at the breakfast island.

"How many babies did she have?"

"Four. It took nearly an hour for her to deliver the first pup. The entire ordeal took almost eight hours. By that time, Kayla went to bed, so there was just me and my mother. Mom had grown up on a farm, so she was familiar with dogs, cats and goats giving birth. She showed me how to clean off the pups and suction their mouths to remove any mucus. It was an experience I never forgot."

"I have read everything I could get my hands on about birthing puppies. I keep telling myself I'm ready for this, but once Buttercup goes into labor, I know I'm going to have to pull it together."

"Buttercup will know instinctually what to do. You just have to let nature take its course."

"Okay, Dr. Ramsey."

Calum pantomimed pulling on a pair of disposable gloves. "You'll just have to stand back and watch me work."

"Speaking of your sister, is she much younger than you?"

"No. We're only ten months apart."

"That's really close."

"Yup. My mother used to tease Kayla and call her an oopsie, because when she went back for her six-week checkup after having me, the doctor told her she was pregnant again."

"Had she planned to have back-to-back babies?"

"No. Soon after that, she and my father separated. They were like yo-yos. They'd break up and reconcile so often that I never knew when I'd come down for breakfast whether he would be gone or whether he'd be sitting at the kitchen table laughing and talking to Mom as if nothing had happened. The one time I asked her about taking him back, she warned me not to interfere. It was the last time I broached the subject with her."

"There are folks that can't live together but keep trying, and those that should never live together."

"Are you speaking from experience, Lucy?"

She opened the fridge, removed a platter with boneless, skinless, thin chicken cutlets, and set it on the countertop. "No, I'm not, because I've never lived with a man."

"Are you opposed to living with one?"

Turning around slowly, she met his eyes. Calum was asking her the same question Johnny had posed. That time, her answer had been only if she were his wife. A month later, he'd proposed, and a week later she'd begun planning for their wedding. In hindsight, she'd wondered if moving in with him during their engagement would've given him less opportunity to sleep with her best friend. But she supposed he probably would have found a way.

"It would depend on the man. Have you ever lived with a woman?"

Leaning forward, Calum rested his forearms on the breakfast bar's granite countertop. "No. That's not to say I didn't come close. Right now, my work schedule doesn't lend itself to living with a woman. My work hours are too erratic to give her as much attention as she may need."

Calum lived alone, while she had Buttercup. Lucy knew when she opened the door, the dog would be there to greet her—if Buttercup wasn't already by her side. She had become her constant and loyal companion. And the closer Buttercup came to having her litter, the closer the date loomed when Buttercup and her puppies would be put up for adoption. Lucy knew it was detrimental to her emotional well-being to become so attached to the dog, yet she couldn't turn her feelings on and off at will when it came to Buttercup.

There are folks that can't live together but keep trying, and those that should never live together. Calum recalled Lucy's words as she opened a cabinet under the countertop to remove a large skillet. She'd admitted she had never lived with a man. Assuming that included her father, he wondered why her parents hadn't been able to stay together.

"Do you have any siblings?"

Lucy's head popped up. "No. I'm an only child. My parents didn't stay together long enough to have more children. They separated when I was six, and were finally divorced the year I turned ten."

Calum recalled one of the photographs with Lucy at her college graduation standing next to a tall man he'd assumed was her father. It was the only photo with him in it. "Are you close with your dad?"

"No. He's more a father than a dad."

"Is there a difference, Lucy?"

She went still. "Yes. Any man can father a child. That is very different from becoming a dad. Even if he and his child's mother aren't together, a real dad makes every effort to be in his kid's life. My father was like Santa Claus—happy to hand out presents but hardly ever coming around. He never skipped on child support payments and, as defined in the divorce agreement, paid my college tuition. He gave me two gifts for my college graduation: a car and the money for a trip abroad—as long as I agreed to take photos of the countries and cities I visited and send him copies. I accepted the car because Gertie was on her last tire and—"

"Gertie?" Calum interrupted.

"Yes, Gertie. Don't you name your vehicles?" No."

"Well, I do. My first doll was named Gertie, and so was my dog. When my grandmother reminded me that Gertie was a girl's name, and the dog was a male, then he became Bertie."

Calum couldn't stop smiling. "Why Gertie?"

Lucy shrugged her shoulders. "I just happen to like the name Gertrude, and so it's Gertie for short."

"You took the car but not the trip?"

Lucy continued seasoning the cutlets. "I told my mother that I was going to send the check back, but she convinced me to keep the check and go abroad because I'd always wanted to enroll in cooking classes in Italy, France and Spain. The trip was great…but no amount of money could make up for everything he'd missed—like my school's annual Father-Daughter Dance, or the trip to college to move me into my dorm room. Each time, it was my mother's brother who stood in for my father."

Calum heard the pain in Lucy's voice when talking about her father, and chided himself for bringing up the subject. He wanted to tell her at least her father was financially supportive, but he doubted that would make her feel better, so he decided against bringing up his own father. She didn't need to know that Keith Ramsey couldn't remain employed for any appreciable length of time because of a problem he'd spent half his life denying.

"Where did you go to college?" he asked, deftly steering the conversation away from her absentee father.

Lucy's expression brightened. "Fisk."

Smiling and nodding, Calum said, "HBCU."

"All the way! I knew I wanted to attend a historically black college or university, and it took me a long time to decide on Fisk."

"Are you a part of the Divine Nine?"

She shook her head. "No. I'd thought about joining a sorority, but never got around to it. I know my mother was disappointed because she went to Howard and rushed Zeta Phi Beta."

Calum watched as Lucy coated the skillet with olive oil, waiting for it to heat up before placing two cutlets in the pan to brown. "If you're going to attend an HBCU, then it goes without saying that you'll join a fraternity or sorority."

"You talk a lot of smack, Calum Ramsey. Did you go to a historically black college, and did you join a fraternity?"

"No, because I got a full academic scholarship to attend Duke, *but* I did join Omega Psi Phi."

"Bragging?"

"No, ma'am," he said, laughing. "Just stating the facts."

Lucy met his eyes. "And the fact is you're very smart."

"I do okay."

"If you got a full ride to Duke, then you're better than okay. Self-deprecation doesn't go along with what you've shown me, and please don't try and deny it."

Calum's jaw tightened as he clenched his teeth. His pet peeve was someone attempting to analyze his personality to put him in a category where they felt they knew who Calum Keith Ramsey was. It had taken years of practice for him to control his emotions, and thereby show people only what they wanted to see.

Chapter Six

"You think you know me that well?"

Lucy blinked slowly. "I only know what I've observed, Calum."

"And what's that?" he spat out.

She glared at him in what had become a stare down. "You have an abundance of confidence. You know who you are and what you want."

"Then you should know I want you for more than just a friend," he countered. Lucy laughed. "What's so funny?"

"You, Calum. I knew you wanted to be more than a friend when you offered to go with me to Furever Paws to choose a foster dog. Then when you drove me on the visits to the vet. And lately, when you started sending me lunch, which I truly love and appreciate."

He angled his head. "So, I'm that transparent?"

"Like glass."

"Well, damn," Calum said under his breath. "I thought I was being subtle."

"Subtlety happens to not be one of your strong suits, handsome."

"Miss Tucker, are you flirting with me?" He repeated the same question she'd asked him the night she gone to Pins and Pints.

A hint of a smile lifted the corners of her mouth. "Yes I am, Mr. Ramsey. Does that bother you?"

Calum stood and came around the breakfast island to stand beside Lucy. He rested his right hand at the small of her back before it inched lower to cradle her hip. "*You* bother me, Lucy Tucker," he whispered in her ear. "You bothered me the day you walked into Pins and Pints and announced you were going to open a bookstore. You bother me every time I walk past Chapter One and see you through the window. And you bothered the hell out of me when you came into the bowling alley in that dress and heels. I wanted to take you home and see what was under the dress that had other men gawking like horny teenage boys. And if I hadn't committed to hiring Aiden, then when he started flirting with you, I would've asked him to leave and never come back. But when you called me 'darling,' he knew he'd overstepped."

Lucy struggled to control the slight tremors of her hand as she speared the lightly browned cutlets with a long-handled fork and placed them on a plate. His hand on her hip sent her emotions whirling as shivers of delight and wanting held her captive.

Calum admitting that she bothered him echoed what she'd experienced whenever they were together. He bothered her during her waking hours and even more when she craved a restful night's sleep. The one time she'd had a dream in which she and Calum were making love, it had left her so shaken she'd buried her face in her pillow to smother the erotic moans threatening to escape from her throat. That was when she'd known she had to stop denying what had become obvious.

Friendship was a pretense, a ploy to conceal her true feelings for Calum.

He removed his hand, allowing her to draw a normal breath. "I'm glad he took the hint because I didn't want to overstep and insult your employee."

Calum pressed a light kiss to her scented neck. "It would never come to that." His fingers caressed her nape. "I'm glad you're enjoying the lunches I fix for you."

This time she couldn't control the shivers eddying through her. Was he aware of what he was doing to her? Her nerve endings were close to short-circuiting.

"You made my lunches yourself?" she asked breathlessly.

Calum's mouth replaced his fingers. "Yep. The first time Timmy brought it over, Cookie made it for you. Then when I told him I wanted you to have soup, he barked at me, saying to make it myself. He claimed he didn't have time to cut up the ingredients that went into soup. I try not to upset my kitchen and bar staff because they're almost impossible to replace. So I started making things for you myself."

"Who taught you to cook?"

"My grandmother. She believed in domestic gender parity. If women worked outside the home and still had to cook, clean, wash and iron, then it should be the same with men. Her teaching me to cook helped me land a job in a diner's kitchen that I used to pay my way through grad school. I worked the night shift and managed to get five hours of sleep before I had to get up and go to class the next day."

"Calum?"

"What is it, bae?"

"You need to stop feeling me up so I can finish dinner."

He pressed his chest to her back. "To be continued."

Lucy blew out a breath. "Thank you."

Calum had spent more than three hours with Lucy, and still he wanted more. The dishes she'd prepared were comparable to those he'd eaten in the best Italian restaurants in Raleigh. She'd admitted to enrolling in two three-week cooking classes to master dishes from Italy's northern and southern regions.

She had excused herself to let Buttercup out into the backyard. Afterward, instead of the dog returning to her bed in the laundry room, she'd found a spot under the dining room table to rest her head on Calum's foot.

"I believe I'm back in Buttercup's good graces."

Lucy lifted the tablecloth and glanced under the table. "Don't move, because she's sleeping."

"I'll have to move before ten because I promised Aiden I'd be back an hour before closing."

"She'll be up before that. Her last walk is around that time. Now, are you ready for dessert? I made tiramisu."

Calum patted his belly. The food had been delicious, as had the beverages. Lucy had concocted a delicious nonalcoholic drink known as Boo Boo's Special. She'd blended pineapple, orange and lemon juices with Angostura bitters and a dash of grenadine, and garnished it with a slice of pineapple and a maraschino cherry.

"I'm going to wait for dessert. After eating so much, this is when I need to go for a walk or take a nap."

Pushing back her chair, Lucy stood. "While you wait for Sleeping Beauty to get up, I'm going to clear the table."

"Don't, Lucy. If you cooked, then I'll clean up."

"You're my guest, so please indulge me."

"Will you indulge me when you come to my place as my guest?"

She stacked several plates. "I thought you didn't engage in tit for tat?"

"Do you remember everything I say?"

"If it's worth remembering, then yes, Calum."

He watched as Lucy made quick work of clearing the table of plates, glass- and silverware. All her movements were graceful, effortless, and he never tired of staring at her. But as beautiful as she was, his interest in her went beyond the physical. When she'd talked about her father, Calum realized another thing they had in common: they were both raised by single mothers. However, the difference was his mother had had to hold down two jobs to keep them from being homeless. If it hadn't been for Calum's grandmother moving in with them, their lives would've been even more chaotic after Keith had left home for good. Meanwhile, Lucy's mother was a college graduate with a career and an ex-husband who provided additional financial stability.

Buttercup came out from under the table, stretching and then shaking before walking slowly in the direction of the pantry. Calum stood. "Sleeping Beauty has awakened."

Lucy dried her wet hands on a dish towel as Buttercup pressed her nose against her leg. "Are you finished cuddling with my boyfriend, or do you plan to go back for another session?"

Buttercup barked in response.

Calum entered the kitchen. "So, I'm your boyfriend?"

"You think not?"

He leaned a hip against the countertop. "You tell me, Lucy."

"If I let a man kiss and feel me up, then yes, he's my boyfriend," she said as she placed dishes on the drying rack.

Crossing his arms over his chest, Calum slowly nodded. "I'm glad we've settled that."

Lucy peered at him over her shoulder. "Wasn't that obvious when I let you kiss me in the bookstore? We both know that if someone saw us, gossip about us would've spread through Spring Forest like Birdie Whitaker's recent breakup with Doc J."

"You're right. There are very few secrets in Spring Forest." He stood straight. "Why are you washing dishes when you have a dishwasher?"

"When my mother gave me the china, crystal and silver as a gift she warned me never to put them in the dishwasher."

"That's quite a gift. What were you celebrating?"

Lucy realized she'd opened Pandora's box and it was too late to retract her words. "I'd just purchased a condo and she wanted to set me up properly. She said she didn't need them anymore since she'd gotten a new set when she remarried." It was a half-truth but there was no reason to reveal they'd been an engagement gift.

Calum's eyebrows lifted questioningly. "Your mother remarried?"

"Yes. And he's wonderful. He owns a construction company. A few months ago, he purchased an old beachfront house on the Outer Banks to use as their vacation home. Once my mother retires from teaching, they plan to live there. She's been an educator for twenty-four years, and her plan is to make it to thirty then retire."

"Why did you decide to give up teaching?"

It was a question she'd asked herself many times. How had she allowed two people to control her life to the point where she'd given up the profession she loved? She would've stayed in Charlotte if the news of Danielle and Johnny's elopement hadn't had her colleagues whispering and pointing fingers. She could have moved away and still been a teacher, but she'd needed a fully fresh start.

"I always wanted to open a bookstore and I told myself if not now, then when? And I don't miss lesson plans and being observed by the principal or assistant principal." This was the truth. She loved teaching and watching children learn, but the school's administration left a lot to be desired. The ones she'd worked with had been more concerned about wielding power than supporting their faculty and staff.

A smile ruffled Calum's mouth. "It is nice working for oneself."

"Copy that," she drawled, grinning.

Calum unfolded his arms. "I think I'm going to take the dessert to go."

"You don't trust Aiden to keep everything running smoothly?"

"It's not about trust, Lucy. I just don't want him to think I've completely abandoned him after only a week on the job."

"I understand." And she did. It had taken Lucy a while to feel comfortable leaving her assistants in the bookstore when she had to leave to feed and walk Buttercup or run errands. "I'll give you enough to share with Aiden." She removed the cake plate from the refrigerator, cutting generous slices of the dessert and placing them in a large glass container with a snap-on top.

"That's too much," Calum protested.

"Yeah right. I'm willing to bet there won't be anything left after you open the top."

"But you didn't leave much for yourself."

"I don't need much. A minute on my lips and forever on my hips," she said in singsong. Dessert was her Achilles' heel. She'd learned to half the recipes and occasionally only use a fourth of the ingredients needed for tarts, muffins or brownies to yield smaller portions. Lucy was taller than the average woman, standing five-eight in bare feet. Eventually, she'd come to accept her height and curvy body; she'd avoided dieting to achieve the impossible. She would never be petite or skinny.

He winked at her. "There's nothing wrong with your hips."

"That's because you like a woman with some meat on her bones."

"Wrong, Lucy. I like you. I like everything about you."

Lucy shoved the container at him. "Go back to work."

"Will you have dinner with me at my place sometime soon? You can bring Buttercup, if you want."

"What day?"

"How about Wednesday?"

"Wednesday's okay. What time should I come?"

"Seven."

Lucy closed the bookstore at six and an hour would give her enough time to come home, shower and change. "If I bring Buttercup, then I'll have to bring her food and bed."

"Don't worry about that," Calum said. "I'll go online and order whatever she needs."

She rested a hand on his arm. "Thank you."

"No, bae. Thank you for a most enjoyable evening."

"Buttercup and I enjoyed having you."

Lucy walked Calum to the door, Buttercup following. She watched him as he got into his SUV and backed out of the driveway. He waved through the open window, and she returned the wave.

"Thank you, sweet girl, for not barking at him." Buttercup barked and Lucy laughed. "I didn't tell you to bark, but it's all right. I know you like Calum as much as I like him." Lucy closed and locked the door. "And I'm glad he's offered to help when you go into labor because having him near will keep me calm. I have everything on the list the vet gave me, so I just hope there won't be any complications."

Lucy had read books on dogs almost obsessively. She had to remember that a dog's instincts took over when whelping and nursing their young. Her job would be mostly stepping back with Calum and letting nature take its course.

And speaking of nature taking its course with Calum…their dinner had just made her even more sure that she wanted more than friendship with him. But there was no rush. She'd wait and see how things went.

Lucy entered the pin number for the cash register and filled the drawers with enough cash and coins to make change for a cash sale. An old-fashioned register had been left at the rear of the store before she'd opened Chapter One, and rather than discard it, she had it positioned on the checkout desk for show. It added to the bookstore's atmosphere of a bygone era.

The bell chimed when the door opened, and she shared a smile with the uniformed man from the shipping company cradling a box against his chest. "Good morning," she said in greeting.

"Good morning. You're in early this morning."

She nodded. "Yes, I needed to get a jump on a few things." Not only had she come in an hour early, but she had also unlocked the door and turned over the sign to indicate she was open for business ahead of schedule.

He set the large box on the counter then tapped a button on his remote device. "I'm so used to leaving your packages at the bowling alley that I almost walked right by."

"And I really appreciate that." As much as she might lecture him for always being at work, it *was* handy that Calum was usually there if a package needed to be signed for. All the carriers knew they could deliver things to the bowling alley if she wasn't around.

"By the way, I thought I saw that orange cat about three minutes ago. You know, the one that's on the missing posters all over town?"

"Oh, you saw Oliver?" Lucy said as she scrawled her signature on his device. There were multiple sightings of the missing cat around the outskirts of the town, yet no one had been able to catch him— much to his nine-year-old owner's dismay.

"He sure is a fast one. When I slowed down and

tried to coax him over to the truck, he took off like a bolt of lightning." He punched a few buttons on his device then gave her a smile. "Nice talking to you, but I gotta go. I have a truck full of packages. You have a good one."

"You, too." He turned and walked out.

Lucy opened a two-drawer file cabinet under the checkout desk and took out a box cutter. Smiling, she removed plastic bags filled with skeins of colorful yarns. Knitting needles in different lengths and sizes ranging from two to eight millimeters were in a portable floral bag. The box also held plastic cases with stitch holders, markers, cable needles, point protectors, row counters, a pair of scissors, a tape measure, beaded pins, a tote storage organizer, and a book with over twenty knitwear designs for dogs of all shapes and sizes. She'd committed to knitting sweaters and pet beds for the upcoming puppy and kitten shower fundraiser for Furever Paws, and now she had everything she'd need.

It had been years since she'd picked up a pair of needles to make a garment. Knitting was certain to revive the memory of when her grandmother had taught her. Grammie, a professional dressmaker, had given up attempting to teach her to sew, but she'd taken to the knitting lessons much better.

She sat on a stool, thumbing through the book. There were patterns for tube coats with rib-, wide- and garter-edged necks. Lucy attached a Post-it on a pattern with a simple coat with straps and another with a front gusset. *I really like this one*, she thought when viewing a vest with a back fastening.

The doorbell chimed and she looked up. "Good morning, Ms. Fowler."

"Good morning, Lucy." The tall, rail-thin woman with graying reddish hair and bright blue eyes pointed to the bags of yarn on the desk. "That looks like quite a knitting project. What's the occasion?"

"I'm planning to knit doggie sweaters for the animal shelter's fundraiser." Lucy filled the tote storage organizer with her purchases and zipped it closed.

"Well, I'm sure you'll do a lovely job. As soon as I put my handbag away, I'm going to check the shelves for misfiled books," Angela announced. She was proud to say, "Once a librarian, always a librarian," and her pet peeve was finding a book filed in the wrong genre.

The phone rang as Angela headed for the office, and Lucy answered it. The caller was a first-grade teacher from the local school who wanted to order an assortment of books as end-of-the-school-year gifts for her students.

Chatting with the woman triggered another idea for Lucy when she thought about decorating the window in the coming weeks. She wanted to highlight summer with beach reads and travel books. After talking with the teacher, she realized it would be useful to also promote summer reading for schoolchildren. Picking up the pen, she listed what she wanted to be included in the ad in the upcoming issue of the *Spring Forest Chronicle.*

She heard Buttercup barking and headed for the office to see her. Walking to the alcove outside the storeroom where she'd set up Buttercup's bed, food and water bowls, she scratched the dog behind the ears.

"What's the matter, baby? You want to go for a walk?" Buttercup barked again, as if in agreement. Reaching for the collar and lead, Lucy fastened it around the dog's neck. "Going for a walk," she called out to Ms. Fowler.

The older woman leaned around a row of shelves. "Okay. I'll cover the front."

Buttercup seemed sprier than she had been in days, pulling on the lead as Lucy quickened the pace. Fifteen minutes into the walk, the dog appeared to tire out, and Lucy headed back to the bookstore where Buttercup lapped up all the water in her bowl, then ambled over to her bed and flopped down.

Lucy watched her foster pet as she closed her eyes. "Soon, little mama. Once those babies are born, you'll have a lot more energy. Five puppies, even though each only weighs around a pound, is enough to slow you down, sweetheart." Leaning over, Lucy pressed a kiss on Buttercup's head. "Rest now, baby girl."

"Do you always talk to your dog?"

Lucy sprang up, startled, to find Calum standing behind her, and cursed herself for not closing the office door. She hadn't seen him since Sunday, and the memory of him kissing and caressing her triggered a longing she hadn't experienced since leaving Charlotte.

"I do on occasion," she admitted. "It calms her."

"Buttercup is the most chill dog I've ever met."

"Oh really? What about when she growled at you?"

"That was only temporary. Now we're besties."

Lucy met the light brown eyes that seemed to see through the façade of indifference she affected whenever they shared the same space. "That's something I'll have to ask her when she wakes up."

Calum handed her the bag he held in his right hand. "Timmy's off today, so I decided to deliver your lunch."

She took the bag, peering inside, smiling. "You made my favorite salad."

"Oh, good, I wasn't sure if you liked salad Niçoise, but I thought I'd give it a try. I cooked the veggies rather than leave them raw."

"I prefer them cooked. Thank you, Calum. I could really kiss you."

Attractive lines fanned out around his jewellike eyes when he smiled. "I wouldn't mind if you did. After all, there's no one here to see us except Buttercup. And now that we're besties, I don't think she'd mind me kissing her foster mama."

"That can't happen here again, Calum. I'm just not ready to advertise to Spring Forest what's been going on between us."

His eyes narrowed. "Are you ashamed to be associated with me, Lucy?"

Waves of shock washed over Lucy with his query. "No. Why would you ask me that?"

He shrugged his broad shoulders. "Just asking."

"There has to be reason why you're asking," she insisted.

"Look, I just came to give you lunch. I'll be expecting you and Buttercup tomorrow at seven."

He turned on his heel and walked out, leaving Lucy staring at his tall, slender physique. She couldn't believe he'd just ceremoniously dismissed her. There were so many questions she wanted to ask Calum, but they would have to wait until the next day.

She couldn't understand why he thought she would be ashamed of him. He was smart, handsome, successful—any woman would be lucky to be with him.

Lucy wanted to tell Calum that she liked him. Liked him kissing her, touching her body. But she'd get a chance to make that clear when she went over to his place. For now, she needed to focus on work. She put the bag with the salad in the minifridge and walked over to the workstation to boot up the computer to design several newspaper ads for the coming weeks.

She made a note to herself that when she was done with business matters, she also had to decide on a house gift for Calum. As a Southern girl, born and raised, she'd been indoctrinated never to show up at someone's house empty-handed. She had less than twenty-four hours to come up with something she hoped he'd like.

Chapter Seven

Calum had called himself a thousand different kinds of fool for questioning Lucy's motives for being with him as he stood in the entryway of his home, waiting for her to arrive.

Strike one, *Ramsey*, he mused. He'd opened his mouth and inserted his foot. Hopefully it would be the last blunder he would make with her. He exhaled when he spotted her Toyota pulling into the driveway.

Calum was out the door as the hatch opened. He lifted Buttercup and set her on the ground. He wasn't certain how Lucy managed to lift the dog in and out of her vehicle without straining herself. Buttercup had to weigh at least sixty pounds. Then, he spotted a ramp between the rear and front seats. It was obvious Lucy used the ramp to get the dog in and out of the Toyota.

He closed the hatch and met Lucy when she got out. His breath caught in his throat as he found himself unable to pull his gaze away from the light-blue-and-white-striped halter top and white cropped slacks. Calum had grown so accustomed to seeing her wearing smocks that it was always a shock—a very pleasant shock—every time he saw her without them. She had wonderfully toned arms and shoulders.

Dipping his head, he brushed a light kiss over her mouth. "Welcome to my home."

Lucy rested a hand on his jaw. "Thank you for inviting me. I bought you a little something." She handed him a small silver shopping bag.

"You know you didn't have to do that."

Going on tiptoe in her white tennis shoes, she pressed her mouth to his, deepening the kiss when his arm went around her waist. Finally, she pulled back to say, "Yes, I did."

"What is it?"

"It's a bowling ball paperweight."

"How appropriate." He kissed her again. "Thank you. Now, let's go inside before my neighbors get jealous."

Lucy glanced around her. "I didn't realize you had a town house this close to downtown."

"I'd originally thought about buying property farther out. However, I changed my mind when negotiating buying the bowling alley. I wanted to be close enough to Pins and Pints to get there quickly in the event of an emergency."

"These town houses are really nice. How long have you lived here?"

"It's been a little more than a year. Before that, I'd rented one of Harris Vega's houses. Come inside, I'll show you around. But don't laugh at how little I've done with some of it. I didn't want this many bedrooms, but the four-bedroom units were the only ones available."

"You may not need the room now, but maybe one of these days you'll be married with children, and you'll need the additional space."

"That's not going to be anytime soon."

"Why does it sound as if you're anti-marriage?"

Calum rested his free hand at the small of Lucy's back as he led her through the entryway and into an expansive space that served as both living and dining room. "I'm not anti-marriage. I'm just not ready for domestic bliss at this time in my life."

Lucy stopped and turned to face him. "Isn't that what you said to that girl you dated in college? But you said that was because you wanted to wait until you knew you could support a wife and a family. Fast forward to present day, and you have a very successful business and live in a beautiful house in a wonderful neighborhood. What's your excuse now?"

He cursed Lucy's incredible recall. The truth was, Lucy was right about him not having a financial excuse for not marrying and/or starting a family. The real reason was fear; fear that he wouldn't know how to be a good husband or father; fear that history would repeat itself. Because, as much as he resented his father, Calum knew it could take just a single crisis for him to possibly end up like Keith Ramsey. If there was any chance he might throw everything away, chasing the bottom of a bottle, then he wanted to make sure there wouldn't be a wife and child left behind to be hurt by his abandonment.

He gave her fingers a gentle squeeze. "This time it could be I haven't met the woman that would make me change my mind."

"It shouldn't be up to someone else to change your mind. Either you want to or you don't. It's just that simple."

"What about you, Lucy?"

"What about me, Calum?"

"Do you want to get married?"

A beat passed. "I'd like to one of these days."

"Have you ever been married?" he asked.

She shook her head. "No."

"Did you come close?"

Another beat passed. "Yes. In fact, I came very close."

Her answer piqued Calum's curiosity. "What happened?"

"He decided we wouldn't make a good couple and moved on."

Lucy seemed uncomfortable, so Calum's gaze shifted to Buttercup as he gave Lucy a moment to pull herself together. He wondered what had happened for Lucy's ex to come to the realization they would be incompatible as husband and wife.

"I'm sorry it didn't work out."

A sad smile flitted over her features. "I'm not sorry, Calum. He did me a favor ending the engagement. If we'd married, it eventually would've ended in divorce." She forced a smile. "I don't want to talk about the past. Are you going to give me a tour of your beautiful home before or after we eat?"

Calum winked at her. "That's up to you. If you're hungry, we can eat now." Lucy looped her arm through his and the brush of her skin against his was like pinpoints of electricity.

"What's on the menu?"

"I'm going to grill red snapper and Mexican street corn. I also made some guacamole. Tonight's featured mocktail is a lemon-limeade made with sparkling water and grenadine."

"You had me at Mexican street corn. If you keep wooing me with food like this, I might just have to hold on to you—at least until another woman steals you away from me."

Is that what happened to you, Lucy? The question popped unbidden into Calum's head. The statement felt a little too pointed, as if it was a sore subject. Had her fiancé ended their engagement to marry someone else?

"No one is going to steal me away, bae. If anyone is going to walk away, then it's you."

A frown creased her forehead. "Why would you say that?"

"Because you'll probably want to marry and have children sometime soon and I still may not be ready to settle down."

"You talk as if I'm in a rush. I'm twenty-seven and I have a while before my biological clock starts ticking. Right now, I'm enjoying my life as it is. My bookstore is doing well and I'm fostering a dog I've come to love, and dating one of Spring Forest's hottest bachelors. Are you blushing, Calum, because I called you hot?"

"I don't blush," he said defensively. "And I don't think of myself as a hot bachelor. Eligible, yes, but definitely not hot."

"Okay, Calum. I stand corrected. I'm happy to say that I'm dating one of Spring Forest's most eligible bachelors."

Calum smiled. "That's better." It was a relief to know that he and Lucy were on the same page when it came to marriage and children. Neither of them was ready for it. "I don't think I've done too badly in the dating department, Miss Lucy Tucker. After you strutted into Pins and Pints wearing next to nothing, dudes couldn't stop talking about how sexy you are."

"You make it sound as if I strolled in wearing lingerie. I did happen to have on a dress."

"A dress that left little to the imagination. I must confess that I had a slight problem falling asleep that night."

"Only slight?" Lucy teased, smiling.

He squeezed her hand again. "You know you're a tease."

Her smile grew wider. "And you like this tease, don't you?"

"You have no idea how much I like you, Lucy."

Calum said "like" when he wanted to substitute the word "love." He knew his feelings for Lucy went beyond a mere liking. He loved her gentleness, her devotion to Buttercup, her patience with the young children that attended the Teddy Bear Storytime, and the peace she radiated that he'd spent most of his life chasing. If they could have a relationship without the undue pressure of insisting on marriage, then that sounded absolutely perfect to him.

"Where did you put Buttercup's things?"

Lucy followed him through the chef's kitchen and down a hallway to the mudroom. Calum had purchased a bed for Buttercup like the one she had in the bookstore, along with a bag of puppy food, several cases of potty pads, and various supplies to have on hand in case Buttercup went into labor.

Buttercup sniffed around the bed and then climbed up on it to lie on her side. Lucy noticed movement against the dog's belly. "Her babies are very active tonight," she whispered.

"Yes, they are. Does she need to be fed?" Calum questioned.

"No. I fed her just before I closed the bookstore. But she'll need water."

Calum reached for a stainless-steel bowl, filled it with water from the sink, and set it down on a rubber mat. "She looks content."

"She's content as long as I'm not too far away," Lucy remarked. "Lately she follows me around like I'm the Pied Piper."

"That's because you spoil her, Lucy. I'll bet you'll do the same when you have children. You'll pamper them constantly and give them anything they want."

Her mouth twisted. "I don't think so. I will not have spoiled children. That will definitely be a no-no."

Lacing their fingers together, Calum led her back into the kitchen. "Just admit it, bae. You're as soft as a marshmallow."

She wrinkled her nose. "I don't like marshmallows."

"You don't like s'mores?"

"Not really."

"I'm willing to bet you'll like my s'mores."

"What makes your s'mores so special?" she asked.

"Just before the chocolate melts completely, I roll them in chocolate chips and crushed peanuts and then put them back on the fire."

"That does sound delicious."

"Believe me, they are. The next time you come, I'll make some for you."

Lucy watched Calum open the built-in stainless-steel refrigerator-freezer and remove a platter with marinated red snapper, and another with ears of corn covered with mayo, chili powder, garlic powder, cilantro and cotija cheese. He set the platters on the quartz countertop and returned to the refrigerator for a bowl of guacamole.

"That's a lot of food for two people, Calum."

"I made enough so you can take home leftovers."

"You're incredible. You already make certain I have lunch, and now it's dinner."

"I can only offer you dinner whenever I have the night off. Aiden and I alternate working the day and night shifts."

"How is he working out?"

"I couldn't have selected a better assistant manager. But then, I always knew he was a good businessman. He was my supervisor when I worked for Harding Investments. He's smart and no-nonsense when on the job, and all of the workers like and respect him."

"Do you think he'll ever live down his reputation as a party animal?"

"Aiden says he's no longer in that life. He likes the quieter vibe of Spring Forest."

"He's not the only one who likes Spring Forest. Of course, living anywhere has its complications. My lease for the rental is up for renewal soon. At that point, I must either purchase the property or vacate it." Lucy was aware that Harris Vega purchased houses to flip and sell. For those that didn't have prospective buyers, he'd offer one-year leases—but the end goal was always to find a permanent buyer.

"Does the lease have a 'rent with an option to buy' clause?" Calum asked.

She tried to recall some of the language in the lease. "I don't think so."

"Not to worry. After I look at your lease, I'll talk to Harris to see if I can get you better terms for your renewal."

"Thank you." She lowered her eyes. "I seem to do that a lot."

"What's that?"

"Thanking you."

Calum came around the cooking island and cradled her face in his hands. "I don't do things for you to thank me."

"Why, then, do you do them, Calum?"

He leaned closer. "Because I like you." He enunciated each word.

Lucy nodded. He liked her and she more than liked him. However, that would remain her secret.

* * *

Lucy opened her eyes when she felt something wet against her ankle. She'd relaxed on a mahogany chair and put her feet up on the matching ottoman—and now her dog had joined her and was staring up at her. She couldn't believe she'd fallen asleep. Stretching her arms, she slumped lower on the chair.

"How was your nap, sleeping beauty?"

"Why didn't you wake me up?"

"I didn't want to disturb you."

She suppressed a moan as she stretched again. After dinner, Calum had taken her on a tour of his home. The exterior belied the expansiveness of the interior with its high ceilings and floor-to-ceiling windows in all the bedrooms. The second-story master suite and the guest bedroom both had en suite baths with soaking tubs, twin vanities and freestanding shower stalls. The master and guest bedroom suites were decorated, but as he had warned, the other rooms were pretty bare. Calum stated he was uncertain what he wanted to do with them. He'd also revealed while at home he spent most of his time on the patio or in the finished basement watching television.

"I ate too much."

Calum left his chair and sat on the ottoman, pulling her bare feet onto his thigh. "You had one fish, one ear of corn and a dollop of guacamole with a couple of glasses of lemonade."

He'd stuffed the snapper with onions, peppers, finely minced garlic and flavored breadcrumbs, and grilled it to perfection. The skin was crispy and the meat moist and flaky. The Mexican corn was the best she'd ever eaten, and the spicy guac triggered a thirst she'd countered with the slushy lemon-limeade.

"Even though everything was delicious, it's more than what I'd normally eat for dinner."

"What do you usually have for dinner?"

"Meat or chicken with a small salad and veggies."

"What about breakfast?"

"I always have coffee with either toast or a muffin."

Calum gave her an incredulous stare. "And lunch?"

She smiled. "Before my fairy godfather began delivering lunch, it was usually leftovers. Every once in a while I'd order something from the Grille."

"You don't eat enough."

"I eat enough to feel full. What I try not to do is overeat."

Calum rubbed Buttercup's back when the dog flopped down next to the ottoman. "I packed up everything to take with you when you go home."

Lucy leaned forward and placed her hand on Calum's shoulder. She felt the warmth of his body under the short-sleeved cotton tee. "Did you save some for yourself?"

"No. Remember I have access to the kitchen in the bowling alley. Most mornings, I go in before

Cookie gets there and I make breakfast and lunch for myself."

"Including my lunch?"

Calum winked at Lucy. "Yes. Including your lunch."

She dropped her hand. "I'm going to leave now. It's time for Buttercup's last walk before she goes to sleep for the night."

"I already walked Buttercup."

"What time is it?"

Calum glanced at the watch on his wrist. "Ten forty."

Lucy was genuinely surprised. "Why did you let me sleep so long?"

"I didn't wake you because you probably needed the sleep. What time do you go to bed?"

"It varies," Lucy admitted. "Some nights I'm in bed around ten. If I'm reading or watching a movie I like, it can be closer to midnight." She held up a hand. "And before you ask, I'm up before six to walk Buttercup. The only day I get to go back to bed after taking care of her is Sunday. That's my day to sleep in a little before tackling laundry and housework. I'll occasionally cook for the week, so all I do when I come home is heat up preprepared dishes."

Calum lifted her bare feet off his thigh. "You know you're going to get even less sleep once Buttercup has her litter."

Lucy nodded. "I know. It'll probably be like getting up in the middle of the night to give a human baby his or her 2:00 a.m. feeding."

"You know you don't have to go home, Lucy," Calum said, standing as she slipped off the chair. "I have an extra bedroom. And don't forget I have food for Buttercup."

"Maybe some other time. I really need to get home and work on my knitting projects." Over dinner, she'd told him about how she'd volunteered to make things for the fundraiser. "I managed to finish one sweater for a little dog or kitty."

"How many do you plan to make?"

"I'm not certain. I bought a lot of yarn, so I'd like to use it all."

The beginnings of a smile tipped the corners of Calum's mouth, bringing Lucy's gaze to linger there. Just looking at that mouth had her remembering when it covered hers, heating her blood like molten lava and reminding her of what she'd been missing as she continued to wallow in a morass of self-imposed celibacy. "What's so funny?"

His smile grew wider. "You."

"What about me?"

"I just can't imagine you knitting."

"Why not, Calum? Would it sit better with you if I told you I spend any free time I have playing games on my phone?"

"No. It's just that…" His words trailed off.

"It's just that you figured a twenty-something woman wouldn't know how to knit. Does your sister know how to knit?"

"No."

"How about your mother, Calum?"

He shook his head. "No. My mother was too busy holding down two jobs to do craftwork—or anything, really, but try and catch up on her sleep."

Lucy was startled by Calum's bluntness. Now she understood why Calum wanted to wait until he was financially secure before marrying and starting a family.

"I didn't mean—" she said in apology.

"I know exactly what you meant." He cradled her face. "I want you to know there's an open invitation for you and Buttercup to hang out here whenever you want."

"I'm willing to bet you'll withdraw that invitation the instant Buttercup's litter starts to poop and pee all over your rugs and beautiful floors."

Calum pressed a kiss to Lucy's forehead. "The rugs can be cleaned, and the floors refinished."

She curled her fingers around his wrists. "That tells me a lot about you."

"And that is?"

Lucy discovered she couldn't think straight with his mouth so close to hers. Close enough to feel his breath feather over her parted lips. "You're going to be a very tolerant father."

He smiled. "Just like you'll be an indulgent mother. Even Buttercup knows how to get one over on you."

She released his wrists. "On that note, I think it's time I head home."

"What's the matter, bae? You can't handle the truth?"

Lucy wasn't about to get into a discussion with Calum about child-rearing. She remembered the ongoing volatile disagreements between her mother and her paternal grandmother about her upbringing that hadn't been resolved to the present day.

"I'd rather not talk about it." She must have gotten through to him because he lowered his hands.

"I'll get the leftovers and help you put Buttercup in your car." His voice was flat, void of emotion.

Lucy didn't want to believe that the evening that had begun so beautifully was ending with an undercurrent of animosity. They didn't share a child or even share in fostering Buttercup, yet they were arguing about something of no consequence to either of them.

She arrived home and set the ramp in place for Buttercup to exit from the cargo area.

"Come on, baby girl. It's time to go turn in for the night." Tail wagging, Buttercup followed Lucy into the house and headed for her bed.

Forty minutes later, Lucy crawled into her own bed. She tossed and turned restlessly, her mind in tumult. She closed her eyes, practicing deep breathing exercises before Morpheus welcomed her in a cocoon of a restful night's sleep.

Chapter Eight

Standing several feet away from Buttercup, Lucy watched the dog pacing and shaking. The change in Buttercup's behavior indicated she was ready to give birth. The day before, she'd taken the dog's temperature. It was below the normal one hundred degrees, which was a sign of the onset of labor. Lucy had mentally prepared herself to remain calm and allow Buttercup's natural instincts to take over, but now that the moment was here, she couldn't help feeling anxious.

She returned to the kitchen, picked up her cell phone and sent Calum a text.

Buttercup has gone into labor.

Lucy stared at the screen, awaiting his response. It came a minute later.

I'll be over after I close. I'll stay with you until all the puppies are born.

Lucy paused and then sent him another message.

Text me when you get here. I don't want you to ring the bell and startle Buttercup. I'll leave the front door unlocked.

Calum sent her a thumbs-up emoji and she replied with a kissy-face one. Knowing she wouldn't be alone when Buttercup delivered her puppies eased some of her anxiety.

Calum stared at the text messages on his phone from Lucy, then noted the time. It was after nine. He'd told her he would come to her house after closing; however, it was Saturday night, which meant Pins and Pints didn't close until 1:00 a.m. Then he had to close out all the cash registers and reconcile credit card purchases.

Drumming his fingers nervously on the desk, he sucked in a lungful of breath, holding it for several seconds before exhaling. Buttercup was in labor, and Calum hoped she wouldn't have her first pup until he got there. He remembered when his sister's dog had gone into labor, and it had taken more than five hours before she'd whelped her first puppy. It was another hour after that before the second one was born. After witnessing the miracle of birth, he'd decided he wanted to become a veterinarian.

When he'd told his mother, she'd smiled and said it was a wonderful profession. She had also cautioned him that getting that degree—or any degree—would require a lot from him in terms of time and money.

Time he'd had. Money he had not. And seeing his mother come home exhausted after putting in twelve-hour workdays triggered a passion for him to find a career where he'd make enough money so she could give up one of her jobs. She worked nine-to-five as a bookkeeper for a trucking company during the day and from eight to midnight as a part-time cashier at a popular chain restaurant off the interstate. Sundays were her days off, in which she slept around the clock. Calum and his sister knew to be quiet so as not to disturb her; fortunately, their grandmother moved in to provide them with adult supervision.

He'd studied hard, graduated high school at sixteen, earned academic scholarships to three colleges and decided on Duke because it was close to home. Some of the bonuses he'd earned from Harding Investments he'd used to pay off his mother's mortgage, which had enabled her to quit her part-time job. For Calum, working in finance wasn't about purchasing top-of-the-line luxury vehicles or designer clothes. It was about becoming financially solvent to the point where he could go into business for himself.

Leaning back in the chair and clasping his hands behind his head, he stared up at the ceiling. He'd worked hard, sacrificed relationships, and it had all paid off—he'd achieved the professional success he'd sought. The next step should be settling down, starting a family...but Calum couldn't quite bring himself to go there.

He was thirty, soon-to-be thirty-one, and was in a better financial state than most. He'd achieved everything he'd ever wanted, but there was still a part of him that seemed to see failure around every corner. His father had been fine until he wasn't. What if that happened to Calum, too? No matter how drawn he'd been to any of the women he'd dated, none of them had ever been able to get him past that fear.

Calum thought about Lucy, remembering when he'd told her he hadn't met the woman who would make him change his mind when it came to marriage. And she'd been right when she'd said *It shouldn't be up to someone else to change your mind.* That was something he had to do on his own.

A knock on the door shattered his reverie. "Who is it?"

"Jake."

Pushing off the chair, he walked over to open it. "What's up?"

"I think we can close down early tonight, boss.

Customers are leaving because there are alerts about a bad storm coming through around midnight. The tornado that hit Spring Forest a couple of years ago still has folks spooked whenever there is a report of high winds."

Calum glanced at his watch again. It was twenty minutes after nine. "Let's see if we can't get everyone out by ten." Closing three hours early would give him more time to spend with Lucy before Buttercup gave birth to her puppies.

Lucy smiled when she saw Calum alight from the Pathfinder. She was surprised when he'd sent her a text that he was arriving in three minutes. As he came closer, she saw the overnight bag, recalling his promise to stay until Buttercup had all her puppies. And that translated into spending the night. He wore a pair of faded paint-spattered jeans, a white tee, and tennis shoes that had seen their better days. It was obvious he'd dressed to assist in birthing puppies.

"Thank you for coming," she whispered. "Did you get Aiden to cover for you?"

"No. We closed early because everyone was leaving to get home ahead of the storm." Calum pressed a kiss to her forehead. "How is Buttercup?"

Lucy closed and locked the door. "She's calmer now. She was peeing a lot, but that stopped. I gave her a little organic yogurt."

Calum set his bag near the door and took Lucy's hand. "Come with me to check on her."

Buttercup lay on her side in the makeshift nesting box, shuddering each time she felt a contraction. Lucy took a step back as Calum went to one knee and gently placed a hand on the dog's side. He glanced up at her over his shoulder. "Inky, Binky, Winky, Dinky and Slinky are taking bets who will get out first."

Lucy gave him an incredulous stare. "That's not their names!"

He flashed a Cheshire cat grin. Lucy was in mama bear mode even before the puppies were born. "So what are they? You said before that you'd already picked them."

"Yes. Because she's so sweet, I've decided her babies should have yummy names."

"What are they?"

"Pancake, Waffle, Fritter, Beignet, Biscuit and Grits."

Calum stood. "You're going to name a boy Beignet?"

Lucy landed a soft punch on his shoulder, encountering rock-hard muscle. "Stop playing, Calum. If she's going to have five or six pups, the odds are she will have at least one girl."

Wrapping both arms around her waist, he pulled her close. "We'll see."

Lucy buried her face between his neck and his shoulder. She didn't think she would ever tire of breathing in his natural scent mingling with the bodywash notes of bergamot, orange and lime. "I was going to make some coffee. Would you like some?"

Calum dropped a kiss on her hair. "Yes. I like mine black and extra strong. I don't mind taking the first shift watching Buttercup while you try and get some sleep." He pressed the pad of his forefinger under one of her eyes. "You look exhausted."

"No, Calum. I'm going to stay up and wait along with you. I'll sleep later."

He hesitated, giving her a long, penetrating stare. "Okay. Together, then."

"Yes," she said, leaning into him for a moment longer. "Together."

Rain and wind slashed the windows as, at the stroke of midnight, Buttercup delivered her first puppy. She bit the membrane covering the puppy, then licked at its nose and mouth, allowing it to breathe. Instinct continued to lead as she nibbled the umbilical cord and then proceeded to lick the puppy's body clean. It was a boy, weighing in at fourteen ounces. Lucy wrote his name—Fritter— on a blue ribbon and attached it around his neck. Fritter was followed a half hour later by a girl. Pancake weighed fifteen ounces. It was minutes before two in the morning when there was another boy—

Waffle—and forty minutes later, Grits, weighing one pound each.

The rain had stopped when the last puppy decided to make an appearance. It was another girl. Calum teased she was the last to be born because, as the runt of the litter, she needed to hang back and eat to catch up with her brothers and sister. Beignet tipped the scale at twelve ounces.

Buttercup had delivered all her puppies within four hours. Lucy and Calum tied the umbilical cord with umbilical tape and cut the cords of two of the puppies with sterilized surgical scissors.

Lucy cleaned the nesting box, discarding the shredded paper, towels, potty pads and disposable gloves in a plastic garbage bag, and then cleaned and lined the space with puppy pads while Calum carefully transferred the golden retriever and her puppies to an extra-large potty-pad-lined bed with raised sides that protected the pups. Buttercup had fallen asleep, along with the litter snuggled against her body.

Lucy shared a smile with Calum. "They can't see or hear, yet they can smell mama's milk."

"You're right about that," he drawled, pulling her close and brushing a kiss on her parted lips. "Birthing puppies is hard work. I don't know about you, but I'm famished. I'm going to take a shower in the half-bath, then raid your fridge."

"You do that while I shower in the other bathroom. I have eggs, bacon and some sausage patties if you want to make breakfast."

"I'll get my bag, then I'll meet you in the kitchen."

"And just leave your clothes on the floor in the laundry room and I'll wash them later." She walked in the direction of her bedroom to shower and change. Birthing puppies was messy, too.

Calum brushed his teeth then stepped into the miniscule shower stall. He shampooed his hair and washed his body twice before reaching for a towel and drying off. It wasn't quite five o'clock, and he planned to eat and then bed down in Lucy's guest bedroom until it was time for him to leave and open Pins and Pints. He slipped into a pair of khaki shorts, a faded blue Duke tee and deck shoes.

He emerged from the bathroom at the same time Lucy walked into the kitchen. Her damp hair hung like strands of curling ribbons around her face and neck. A pair of black yoga pants and a matching tank top molded to her curvy body like a second skin. Calum forced himself not to stare at her breasts as he turned to open the refrigerator, wondering if she was oblivious to her effect on him.

"Do you have any ingredients for omelets?" His voice was muffled as he pushed his head as far as he could into the fridge to get himself together. Calum couldn't understand how Lucy was able to twist him into knots like a bumbling adolescent boy. What was he? A mature man or a horny teen?

"Yes. If you look in the vegetable drawer, you should find peppers, chives, spinach, mushrooms and herbs. There's also cheese in another drawer."

Calum glanced at Lucy over his shoulder, feeling as if he'd maintained a modicum of self-control. "I found some diced ham. Do you want the ham instead of bacon?"

"Yes. Is there anything I can help you with?" Lucy questioned.

He gave her a warm smile. "I don't think so, bae."

"I can cut up some melon," she volunteered.

"That sounds good."

Calum and Lucy moved about the small kitchen like a matador sidestepping the bull, their bodies innocently touching when he reached up to remove a bowl from the overhead cabinet. Her hand grazed his forearm as she opened a drawer under the countertop to retrieve a melon baller. The kitchen in the town house was large enough for at least four people to move around freely without bumping into one another—but the galley kitchen at Lucy's house was another matter. Working side-by-side and occasionally touching each other was as intimate as dancing close. A slight caress, bump, or even an intentional touch, ignited all of Calum's senses.

He smiled. "I didn't think the melon would be this fancy," he said teasingly.

Lucy bumped him with her hip. "There's something kinda sexy about eating a grape and savoring the juice literally popping into your mouth. It's the same when you bite into a melon ball. You get to enjoy the both the juice *and* the meat of the fruit."

Calum gave her a sidelong glance. "I never think of food in that way. I just eat it."

"Think about it, Calum. It's the same with drinking wine. You take a swallow, hold it in your mouth for several seconds while savoring the notes from the grapes on your tongue, then you let it slide down the back of your throat."

Throwing back his head, Calum laughed. "I'm beginning to think you spent too much time in Italy."

"That's where I learned to not only respect what chefs prepared but also enjoyed it more—including what they serve it in. Wine is not pop or beer. It's not to be guzzled."

Picking up a knife, he quickly diced peppers and chopped herbs for the omelets on a cutting board, scraping them into a bowl before opening a glass container with diced ham. "I wouldn't know about wine because I don't drink it."

Lucy went completely still. "You've never drunk wine?"

"Nope." He paused. "Actually, I take that back. I've had champagne."

"I'm puzzled, Calum."

"What about?"

"Are you saying you never drink?"

"When I do drink, it's usually a nonalcoholic beer.

I like the taste of beer but there's no way I can issue a directive that the bowling alley's employees are not permitted to drink on the job if I break the rule myself."

"Do they follow your directive?"

"I believe they do. They are aware if they're caught, then it's either suspension without pay or termination. I can't be a cop, Lucy, and breathalyze my workers. I operate on a trust system and so far, it seems to be working."

Lucy continued scooping balls from halved cantaloupe and honeydew. "After Buttercup weans her puppies and they all are adopted, I plan to visit Pins and Pints to bowl a couple of games."

"You bowl?"

Lucy realized Calum didn't know much about her. In fact, most people in Spring Forest only knew her casually, and that's what she liked. She'd moved from Charlotte to escape ridicule and embarrassment. She'd chosen to leave the past behind when she'd relocated to Spring Forest.

To those curious enough to ask her about herself, she'd revealed she was a former teacher. She'd discuss casual things—where she went to school, how she was enjoying fostering a dog. Most other things, she kept to herself. Except with Calum. She found herself telling him all sorts of things—trusting him with much more than she'd trusted anyone with since leaving Charlotte behind.

"Yes, Calum, I do bowl. Why do you think I wouldn't?"

"I don't know. I suppose it's because I know so little about you."

Lucy wanted to tell Calum that he'd read her mind. Instead she said, "What you see is what you get, sweetheart."

Calum leaned into her. "Before I was 'darling' and now I'm 'sweetheart'?"

She scrunched up her nose. "You can be whatever you want."

"Well, damn," he drawled, the two words pregnant with amusement. "You've left the door wide open with that statement."

Lucy giggled. "Should I be afraid?"

"Nah, beautiful. I think you'll be able to handle whatever happens between us."

"Aren't you going to give me a hint?"

She liked their witty banter. That was something she'd never experienced with Johnny. Most times she'd found him much too serious. For him, life was a puzzle, and he always acted like he hadn't quite found all the pieces. It had led to a gloomy outlook, with him always assuming that the real picture— whatever it was—held something disturbing. For example, when he'd been chosen to join one of Charlotte's top law firms, he'd refused to believe it was because of his brilliant legal mind. Instead, he'd thought the firm's partners were hiding their real motives and that they'd only wanted to hire him because the company needed to appear more diverse and inclusive. Surely it must be for the hidden motive and not because he'd graduated number one in his law school class and achieved a near perfect score on the bar exam.

Lucy hadn't realized how tired she'd gotten of his complaints and insecurities until after their breakup. Now in hindsight, she knew if she had married Johnny she would've been relegated to constantly being a cheerleader or life coach, spending most of her time continually encouraging him and boosting his ego.

"No," Calum said after a comfortable silence, "because I believe in letting things unfold naturally. When you force events, they never end well."

Lucy agreed with Calum on that point—especially where it concerned their relationship. She liked dating him, spending time with him. She wasn't sure how far she was ready for this relationship to go, but she was willing to see what path it took.

Lucy maneuvered around Calum to get two small bowls for the fruit. She filled one, speared a melon ball and extended the fork to Calum. "Taste this."

He took the melon between his teeth, bit into it and chewed slowly before swallowing. "I see what you mean about getting a mouthful of juice. Do you think this why we see paintings of nobles being fed grapes?" Lucy gave him another piece. "It is kinda sexy to be hand-fed."

Lucy patted his back. "Don't get too used to it, sport."

"This is something I could get very used to," he said, wiggling his eyebrows.

And I could get very used to cooking with you. Though their relationship was still very new and undefined, she liked where it was heading. With him, there was no pretense that had her second-guessing or looking for an ulterior motive. He was confident and forthcoming, while he hadn't hesitated when expressing his views on marriage and becoming a father. She had hit the jackpot with him.

Lucy sat next to Calum at the breakfast island, savoring bites of a herb, ham and cheese-infused omelet, suppressing a moan with each forkful. "This omelet is delicious."

"I'm glad you like it. I've lost count of how many different varieties I made when I'd worked at the diner."

"Which one did most people order?" she asked between sips of coffee.

"The Western or Denver omelet. Mushroom and spinach were close seconds."

"I think you missed your calling, Calum."

He dabbed the corners of his mouth with a napkin. "Why would you say that?"

"You are an incredible cook. The lunches you prepare for me—not to mention the grilled fish, corn
and guacamole you made the other night—surpass
what I've eaten in some of the finest restaurants. So,
why didn't you open a restaurant instead of owning
a bowling alley?"

"Firstly, I'm not a trained chef. And secondly, I
did the research and discovered many new restaurants do not survive their first year."

"But couldn't you hire a trained chef? Or get some
training yourself?" Lucy questioned. "And it's not as
if you don't know how to run a business."

"That's true, but Spring Forest has Veniero's and
the Main Street Grille, and a few cafés and bak-
eries. It didn't need another eating establishment.
Meanwhile, the bowling alley was in disrepair and
the former owners were looking to sell. I saw an
opportunity. It's been three years and business has
been great."

"I'll admit," Lucy replied, "I was worried about
opening a bookstore in a town where one had gone
out of business. I kept telling myself if the other one
didn't survive, there was no guarantee Chapter One
would. But I had a vision for it that I really wanted
to bring to life."

"And you've done an amazing job. The store is
beautiful and welcoming, and your window displays
are works of art. I have to admit I did take photos of
your Halloween and Christmas displays because I

wanted an idea how I can decorate the bowling alley this year to give it a festive feel."

"I can help you out with that," Lucy volunteered. "Fall and winter holiday decorations will be in stores in a couple of months, and then you can decide what you want." She smiled when Calum breathed a kiss on her hair.

"Thank you, sweetheart."

"You're welcome," she crooned. "I'm going to clean up the kitchen and then check on Buttercup."

Calum slipped off the stool. "I'll help you."

This time Lucy didn't reject his offer when they made quick work cleaning up the remains of breakfast. She stood next to Calum, holding hands as they watched Pancake and Beignet nurse while their brothers slept. "She's proud of her new family," Lucy whispered. It was obvious Buttercup had mated with another golden retriever. All the puppies resembled their mother.

"They are a good-looking litter. It's going to be easy for the shelter to find forever homes for Buttercup and her pups."

Lucy felt as if she'd been doused by a bucket of ice-cold water when Calum mentioned adoption. She didn't want to think of coming home and not having Buttercup greet her and listen to her lengthy monologues. The gentle, sweet golden retriever had filled a void in her life she hadn't known she had until she'd moved to Spring Forest.

The tears filling her eyes overflowed as she struggled to keep raw emotions in check. Lucy clapped her free hand over her mouth to muffle the sob trapped in her throat that threatened to escape and embarrass her. "I don't want to lose her," she whispered over and over.

Calum gathered Lucy against his chest and ran a hand up and down her back. "It's all right, bae. You're not going to lose Buttercup." He buried his face in her hair. She'd warned him that it was going to be difficult for her to give up her foster once the puppies were weaned. However, that wasn't going to happen for weeks.

"When I signed the foster agreement, I knew I would have to give her up," Lucy said, her voice muffled against his chest. "I feel like I'm watching the countdown for a bomb to go off, except instead of an explosion, it will be me giving up something I've come to love."

Calum cupped her chin, raising her face. Lucy had lied about crying ugly. Tears had spiked her lashes and the flush suffusing her light brown complexion made it appear like a rich, sun-ripened peach.

Lowering his head, his lips brushed against hers in a slow, gentle healing. First, it was her mouth, then her eyes, before he trailed light kisses along the column of her silken neck then returned to taste the sweetness of her lush lips. "Everything's going to be all right," he said.

"Will it?" she said between trembling lips.

"Of course. I promise." Calum wasn't certain whether it was an empty promise, but it was the only thing he could think of to comfort her. He smothered a groan as Lucy pressed her breasts against his chest and he felt the beginning of an erection.

He'd waited more than a year denying what had been obvious the first time he'd seen Lucy Tucker. It had been more than three hundred and sixty-five days of rejecting advances from women who'd made it known they were interested in him; countless nights of waking up from erotic dreams with him making love to Lucy, forced to take frigid showers to wait for his erection to go down. Nothing mattered in that instant but the woman in his arms.

Lucy realized she wanted him. She wanted what she'd been missing, and she finally felt ready to fill another void in her life that had been empty since moving to Spring Forest. His kisses had aroused a passion she had long forgotten existed. Everything about him pounded the blood in her veins, made her heart beat a double-time rhythm, and her knees tremble.

"Calum, please."

"Please what, bae?"

Heat swept over her from head to toe. "Don't make me beg you to make love to me."

It was the last thing she said before he swept her up in his arms and carried her to the bedroom. No words were needed as their bodies did the talking for them. Calum relieved her of her clothes in under a minute, his following, and when she opened her arms and legs to him, she bit her lip to keep from crying out at the pure pleasure of feeling him inside her.

The heat from his large body, the sound of his heavy breathing in her ear, had awakened her dormant sexuality and she rose to Calum in a moment of uncontrolled passion that shattered her into a million little pieces.

Calum knew the wait had been more than worth it as the heat from Lucy's body was transferred to his, growing hotter and hotter until his body refused to follow the dictates of his brain. Lucy was offering him the most exquisite lovemaking he'd ever experienced. It was as if she held nothing back. Their bodies were so attuned with each other, he knew exactly when she was going to climax.

Burying his face in the pillow cradling her head, he groaned out his release, holding the mound of feathers in a death grip as he collapsed heavily on her. Seconds later, he rolled off her body and they lay like spoons. Once their breathing returned to a normal rate, they fell into a sated sleep reserved for lovers.

Chapter Nine

Lucy woke with a start when she heard barking. As she scrambled to get out of bed, she felt slight discomfort—a stretch in muscles that hadn't been used for a long time. Then she saw something on her inner thighs; it was blatant evidence that they'd been so caught up in the moment last night that Calum had made love to her without using a condom. Dampening down the panic roiling through her, she found the tee Calum had discarded and pulled it over her head.

"Where are you going?"

She refused to look at Calum. "Buttercup is barking, and I need to see what she wants."

Walking on bare feet, Lucy half walked, half ran to see her dog. Buttercup had gotten out of the bed and was standing near the back door. It was a sign that she had to go out. Lucy opened the door to let her out into the backyard, then returned to check on the puppies. They were awake, rooting around the bed, while making whining noises.

Lucy gathered several clean potty pads from a package, and gently moved the puppies to one corner of the bed while she replaced the soiled ones. She'd just finished cleaning and filling Buttercup's water bowl when the dog barked to be let in. She also half filled the food bowl, hoping Buttercup would feel like eating after her early morning ordeal.

"How is she doing?"

This time Lucy did turn around to face Calum. He'd put on his shorts. She stared at the stubble on his lean jaw. "She appears to be doing quite well." Buttercup had lapped up the water and then returned to the bed where her puppies were rooting to find a teat.

"I think we have to talk." His tone was flat.

Nothing in his expression revealed the anxiety she'd managed to quell when seeing to the needs of the dogs. Now that she was fully awake and thinking of the calendar, she realized that she and Calum had picked the wrong time of the month to have unprotected sex.

"Yes, we do," she said as she led the way into the kitchen. Squaring her shoulders, Lucy gave him a steady stare. "I've never had unprotected sex before, Calum."

He blinked slowly, crossing muscular arms over his bare chest. "Neither have I."

"I should've told you that I'm not on birth control."

"I should've asked. Especially since I didn't bring any condoms with me."

"Well, I supposed that makes two of us not being responsible."

Calum lowered his arms, his hands curling into fists. "This is not about playing the blame game, Lucy. I'm not going to lie and say I didn't want to make love with you. That was something I've wanted to do for a long time."

She had to admit, she felt the same way. And last night had been amazing—better and more fulfilling than any sex she'd had, even with the man she'd thought she was going to marry. But she'd only just worked up her courage to be intimate with a man again. She wasn't sure she was ready for more. And a baby would be a *lot* more.

She knew they needed to talk about this, but right now, Lucy really wanted him to leave so she could get her thoughts in some semblance of order. Her emotions were in tumult because if she was pregnant, then her entire life would change.

"If you are pregnant, I want you to know I'll be here for you."

It was the right thing for Calum to say and Lucy was glad to hear it…but on the other hand, could she really believe it? "You'll be here for me if I decide to have your baby?" Lucy repeated. "But you told me in no uncertain terms that you're not ready for fatherhood." Would he make a commitment only to back out when push came to shove? Was he like Johnny after all? And like her father, too? She didn't want to believe it…but only time would tell.

A beat passed. "I will accept the responsibility of fathering a child whether planned or unplanned. In other words, I will have to step up and get ready."

It wasn't exactly *I'm here for you no matter what, bae*, but it was better than nothing…wasn't it?

She sucked in a breath and then let it out slowly. There was so much she needed to sort through—her feelings, her fears, her plans for the future and how this would impact them. But perhaps she didn't need to tackle all of that right away. After all, maybe they were being premature. There was no need to talk something into existence. "We're debating something that may not happen."

"Either way, will you let me know one way or the other?"

Lucy fought to hide a flinch at his businesslike tone. Where was the man who'd made love to her the previous night? "Yes, Calum. I will let you know."

He glanced at the microwave clock. "I'm going to head out now. I need to go home and get ready for work. I'm off at six, so I'll swing by and check on Buttercup and the puppies."

Lucy gathered her courage and then took a step forward to rest her forehead on his shoulder. She felt some of the tension ease from him, and she relaxed in turn. The connection between them was still there, even if last night had muddled things up. With time, though, she thought maybe they could work things out, find a way forward.

But for now, she needed some time to herself to figure out what she wanted to come next. She pulled back. "Please don't. I'm going to plan how to take care of the dogs and make sense of what happened today."

Calum cupped the back of her head. "Are you asking me to stay away?"

"Yes. But only for a while."

His eyes searched hers for a long moment, but then he nodded. "Okay. I'll give you your space."

"Thank you."

Lucy didn't have to wait long to discover what she'd suspected when she missed her period several weeks later. The readout on the wand of the home pregnancy test indicated she was pregnant. It was the second test she'd taken that week, and she'd hoped beyond hope it was a false positive.

Calum had kept his promise to keep his distance, which wasn't an easy feat since their businesses were so close by. While he didn't visit himself, Timmy continued to bring the lunches Calum prepared for her.

Reaching for her phone, she tapped a number in her contacts.

"What do I owe the honor of this call from my prodigal daughter?"

"Stop, Mom. It's not *that* strange for me to call. You know we talk to each other a couple of times a month."

"A couple of times a month isn't enough from my only child."

Lucy crossed her bare feet at the ankles. "You know I don't do well with guilt." The news she had to share was right on the tip of her tongue, but she couldn't quite manage to say it. To stall, she asked, "How's the love of your life?" Silence followed her query. "Are you blushing, Mom?"

"No."

"Yeah, you are. After all, you were the one that told me Roosevelt Lewis is the love of your life."

"I must have been drinking when I told you that."

"You don't drink. There's no need to be embarrassed about being in love with your husband. By the way, how is he?"

"Well. He's at the beach house updating the electricity. I keep telling him there's no rush to fix up the place because I have another six years before I put in for retirement."

"Have you considered teaching for twenty-five years instead of thirty? That way you'll have four additional years to spend in retirement with your husband. And it's not as if you need the money. You claim Roosevelt has enough money to last you both into old age."

"Now you sound like Roosevelt."

"That's because my stepfather is a very wise man. Imagine all of the fun you'll have when your grandchildren come to spend the summers."

"I really like that Roosevelt's grandchildren think of me as their grandmother. But nothing would make me happier than if my daughter gave me a biological grandchild."

She'd had a feeling her mother would say that. Ever since marrying Roosevelt and becoming a stepgrandmother, she'd been dropping hints about wanting to spoil Lucy's babies, too. But would she feel the same way when it was reality and not just an idea?

Lucy beckoned Buttercup closer when she stood in the doorway to her study, wanting the comfort of the animal's presence and support. The dog came in and flopped down for Lucy to scratch her behind the ears. Poor Buttercup looked tired—and no wonder. The puppies tended to nurse around the clock. Lucy had to continually refill the water bowl and give Buttercup three to four small meals a day to keep her strength up. She made a mental note to order an automatic pet feeder and fountain, which would make the process easier. It was another reminder of how much time and care newborns required—of any species.

"That's why I'm calling, Mom. You're going to get

your wish. I'm pregnant." Only the sound of breathing came through the earpiece. "Mama? Are you still there?"

"Yes," came a strangled whisper. "Did you say you're pregnant?"

"I took a couple of home pregnancy tests, and the results are the same. I have an appointment to see an obstetrician next week."

"How? Who?"

Lucy smiled. "I shouldn't have to tell you how. My baby's father owns a business a couple of doors from mine."

"Do you intend to marry your baby's father, Lucy?"

"No." She'd done some soul-searching over the past few weeks, and this was one decision she was sure of. Calum might offer, or he might not, but either way, she knew what her position was. "I will not marry a man just because I'm carrying his child. I won't put myself or my baby through having him throw that up in my face whenever he loses his temper." Lucy clapped a hand over her mouth once she realized what she'd said. "I'm sorry, Mama. I didn't mean for it to come out like that."

"Don't apologize, Lucy. If I'd had your resolve, it would've saved me years of grief."

"Don't forget you were given a second chance at love when you married Roosevelt Lewis."

"You're right about that."

"I'm glad you found someone worthy of your love."

"What about you, Lucy? Is the father of the baby you're carrying worthy of your love?"

Lucy froze. She hadn't expected her mother to ask her that. Especially when she still wasn't sure what her feelings were. Did she love Calum? Or was she falling in love with him?

"To be honest, Mom, I don't know."

"You slept with a man you don't trust to be worthy of you? Or is it that you're not sure you love him?"

"It's not that. He's a good man, and we do have feelings for each other," Lucy countered. She recalled Calum saying he'd wanted her for more than just a friend.

"How long have you known this man, Lucy?"

She heard the hysteria in Myra's voice. "We've been friends for more than a year."

A sigh came through the earpiece. "That sounds better."

"But I still don't intend to marry him just because I'm carrying his baby."

"And you don't have to, sweetie. If I'd had your strength when I found myself pregnant, I wouldn't have had to deal with the mother-in-law from hell."

"Grandmother is who she is, and I doubt if she will ever change." Her father's mother was an angry, condescending and vindictive woman from whom Lucy kept her distance.

"I forgot to ask how you are feeling?"

"I'm okay."

"Just okay, Lucy?"

"Yes."

There was no need to tell Myra that her breasts were tender and she tired easily, because knowing her mother, she would take a leave of absence from her teaching position and drive from Charlotte to Spring Forest to stay with her until she delivered the baby.

"Okay, I'm going to take your word that you're fine. But if you need me, I'll put in for a leave and stay with you."

Do I not know my mother? Lucy thought. "I'll call you again after I see a doctor."

"I'll be here. I love you, baby girl."

Lucy felt a rush of tears prick the backs of her eyelids. "I know, Mom. I love you, too."

She hung up before she could become even more emotional. Lucy didn't know what was wrong with her. It wasn't just the hormone flux from the pregnancy. Ever since fostering Buttercup, her moods had vacillated sharply between highs and lows.

She didn't use to be that way. Even when she'd discovered Johnny and Danielle had run off together, she'd reacted like an automaton. She'd calmly asked her mother to let the invited guests know the wedding was cancelled and the return of gifts was forthcoming. And if she'd felt anger or rage, it was directed at her fiancé for his betrayal and her best friend for her deceit. Lucy had bottled up those feelings as she focused on planning the next phase of her life.

And now that life was about to change. It would take only a few months for people to know that the owner of the bookstore was carrying the owner of the bowling alley's baby. She was nervous about telling Calum, much less everyone else. She decided that conversation could wait until after she'd seen a doctor.

Eager for a problem that she could easily solve, Lucy booted up her laptop and searched pet stores for what she needed for Buttercup. It took less than fifteen minutes to place an order for a pet fountain with a capacity for a gallon of water, and a programmable automatic feeder. She paid extra for expedited shipping for the items to be delivered to the bookstore the following day.

Life was getting easier for her foster, while hers was becoming more complicated.

Lucy had asked Calum to give her space, and that's exactly what he'd done for several weeks.

But enough was enough. He had spent too many sleepless hours wondering if he was going to be a father. There were times when he wanted it to be true, then others when he felt certain he wasn't ready to raise a child when he still had unresolved issues about his own father. Walking out of his office, he told the young woman behind the bar to pick up the calls because he was going out for a while.

Calum opened the door to Chapter One and came face-to-face with Angela Fowler. "Good afternoon, Ms. Fowler."

The former librarian smiled. "Good afternoon, Calum. How can I help you?"

"Is Lucy in?"

"Yes, but she's in the back."

"Is it possible for me to see her?"

Ms. Fowler clasped her hands together in a prayerful gesture. "I don't think so."

Calum glared at the woman. "And why not?"

The older woman averted her eyes. "She's a little under the weather. I think she's coming down with something."

Something...like morning sickness? "Just let me check on her," Calum said, making his voice as persuasive as possible. "I promise I'll go if she tells me to."

She looked him up and down, as if deciding whether or not to trust him. Finally, she must have decided in his favor because she headed toward the rear of the store and unlocked the door to the office. "Thank you, Ms. Fowler."

She just nodded in reply.

Calum entered the office and looked for Lucy. She wasn't in the kitchen area. He walked down the narrow hall toward the bathroom and that's when he heard movement behind the slightly ajar door.

He opened it and saw Lucy on her knees hovering over the commode, retching. The sound of her gagging paralyzed him for several seconds. Then he was galvanized into action, rushing over to hold her hair off her face while he waited for her to finish purging her stomach.

He pulled paper towels off a rack, wet them in the basin and, sinking down to the floor, he gently cleaned her face. Her eyes were red and tears streamed down her cheeks.

Cradling the back of her head, he gently pulled her against his chest. "When were you going to tell me?" he whispered in her ear.

"I wanted to wait until I saw a doctor."

Calum breathed a kiss on her scalp. "When's that, bae?"

Lucy sighed. "Next week."

"Are you pregnant?" He asked her the question that had plagued him for weeks.

She nodded. "I'm almost certain. I took two home pregnancy tests and both were positive."

He smiled despite the seriousness of the situation. "Does that mean we're having twins?"

Pushing against his shoulder, Lucy stood and went to the sink to take cup from a dispenser. She filled it with water and rinsed her mouth. "That's not funny, Calum."

He rose to stand. "I'm sorry, Lucy. I was just trying to lighten the mood and make you laugh."

Lucy took another paper towel, wet it and pressed it to her eyes. "Right now, I don't feel like laughing."

Calum sobered. "How long have you been throwing up?"

"This is the first day. I was feeling a little queasy before I had lunch, but it wasn't until a few minutes ago that I felt sick."

"Do you think Ms. Fowler can handle the store for while?"

"Why?"

"Because you need to go home and rest. I'll come with you and make something light that hopefully you'll be able to keep down."

Lucy was too drained to reject anything Calum offered. She was tired. No, she was exhausted. It didn't matter if she slept for six, eight, or even ten hours—she still woke exhausted. The baby was sapping her energy and nutrition. She'd eat and then in no time, she'd feel hungry again.

"Okay, Calum." The two words were filled with resignation.

"Do you mind if I tell Ms. Fowler to take over for you while you're out?"

"Yes, please. Let her know I'll be back in time for the Teddy Bear Storytime."

"Do you think you'll be up to that?" Calum questioned, giving her a skeptical look.

"I think so." She certainly *hoped* so. Lucy knew

barfing in front of children would no doubt trauma-tize them. She discarded the paper towels in a nearby wastebasket. "Let me talk to her."

She left the office and walked to the front of the store. Ms. Fowler had just tallied a purchase and handed an elderly man a bag with his books, but she turned to Lucy in concern. "How are you feeling?"

"A little better, thank you. I'm going home to rest for a while. If I don't get back in time for the read aloud, do you think you can fill in for me?"

"Are you kidding me?" Ms. Fowler said excit-edly. "Of course, I will. Now you go home and get some rest," Ms. Fowler added, affectionately pat-ting her back. "Don't you worry about anything but feeling better."

Calum looped an arm around Lucy's waist. "Someone from the bowling alley will be over to set up the chairs for you."

"Thank you, Calum."

"You're welcome, Ms. Fowler."

"Ms. Fowler seemed very concerned about you," Calum commented once they were in his car. "Did you tell her about the baby?"

"No, Calum. You're the only one besides my mother that knows."

He gave Lucy a quick glance. "You told your mother?"

"Of course. She has a right to know that she's going to be a grandmother."

"Does this mean you intend to have the baby?"

"Of course. But what about you? Do you want this baby, Calum? Do you want to be part of his or her life?"

"What the hell kind of question is that to ask me? Of course, I want the baby. Neither of us planned on becoming parents during this time in our lives, but I will not allow our child to grow up believing we didn't want him or her. And I'd like for you to let me know when you're going to the doctor because I want to go with you."

Lucy rested her left hand over his right one on the steering wheel. "I will let you know. And you're right. Regardless of whether we stay together, I want our son or daughter to know they're loved."

Calum clenched his teeth. He'd told Lucy before that he'd take responsibility for his child, but apparently she hadn't believed him. She didn't know that he'd grown up with his father in and out of his life like a revolving door—she didn't know how committed he was to making sure he never put his own child through that.

On the other hand, while Lucy's childhood hadn't been as dysfunctional as his, she had grown up with divorced parents. Calum swore an oath. It was time to end another generation of absentee parents.

Chapter Ten

"Ms. Tucker, the doctor will see you now. Mr. Tucker, please wait here," the nurse told Caleb as he stood up with Lucy. "Dr. Reid will meet with you after he sees your wife."

Caleb had accompanied Lucy to Raleigh for her first appointment with an obstetrician. When the nurse called him "Mr. Tucker," Lucy went completely still. A barely perceptible shake of his head was enough for her not to correct the woman. There were other husbands in the waiting room with their pregnant wives and no doubt he'd been grouped together with the other men.

He pressed his mouth to her ear. "We'll talk about this later." She nodded and then followed the nurse.

He stared at Lucy until he lost sight of her when she disappeared behind a closed door.

"I'm willing to bet this is your first one."

Calum stared at a slightly balding man sitting a few feet away. "Are you speaking to me?"

The man nodded. "Yes. Is this going to be your first baby?"

Extending his legs, Calum slumped lower in his chair. He wanted to tell the man to mind his business, but he didn't want to be rude—especially since he had no idea how long they'd be stuck here together. "How did you know?" he asked instead.

"You seem antsy. This is my third rodeo and I've learned to analyze potential fathers just by their body language."

"And mine?" Calum questioned.

"You're wound so tight that with one more turn you'll shatter into a thousand pieces. Lighten up, man. She's going to be okay."

There was no doubt Lucy would be okay. Calum wasn't nearly as certain about himself. Not only was he wound tight, but he was also frightened. Before meeting Lucy, he'd believed he'd had his life together with a new home and thriving business. That changed the instant she'd walked into Pins and Pints and introduced herself.

Calum knew it wasn't only her beauty that had attracted him. He'd found himself intrigued as to why a single woman would move to Spring Forest to open a business when everything about her screamed big-city sophistication.

He'd spent more than a year befriending her while hoping their friendship would evolve into a more intimate relationship. Well, his wish had come true. He just hadn't anticipated it would take only one spin of the baby-making roulette wheel for them to hit the jackpot.

When Lucy had asked him if he wanted the baby, he'd told her he did. And he'd meant it. But what he truly wanted was to be a good father to his child, and he wasn't sure he knew how. Swallowing down his fear, Calum forced himself to think rationally. He had time to learn to become a good father.

Calum smiled at the chatty man. "You're right. She will be okay."

"The first time my wife told me she was pregnant, I freaked out. At that time she was just my girlfriend. I met her in grad school, and we had enough student loans to sink the *Queen Mary*, but I knew I had to step up and do the right thing. We went to the justice of peace and got married. Meanwhile, I had a tiny off-campus studio apartment that was no bigger than a closet and we lived there until she had the baby. By that time, I'd graduated and gotten a position with a tech company that paid me well enough for us to rent a small house. Julie's widowed mother came to live with us, and she took care of the baby while Julie found a job."

"It sounds as if you guys worked everything out."

"Thankfully we did. Our oldest son is six and he just finished the first grade. The younger one celebrated his third birthday last month. Julie and I decided to try for one more baby, hoping this time it would be a girl."

Calum's eyebrows lifted questioningly. "Is she having a girl?"

"Yep!"

"Congratulations."

"Thanks, man." He extended his hand. "I'm Gavin Walsh."

Calum shook the proffered hand. "Calum Ramsey."

"It's nice meeting you, Calum."

The door opened and the nurse reappeared. "Mr. Tucker, the doctor will see you now. Your wife is in room four."

He stood up. "Good luck, Gavin."

"You, too."

Calum walked down the carpeted hallway until he came to the room where Lucy sat facing a white-coated doctor who didn't look old enough to shave. The doctor held out his hand. "I'm Dr. Reid—pleasure to meet you."

"Calum Ramsey."

"Please sit down, Mr. Ramsey."

Calum took a seat beside Lucy and reached over to grasp her hand.

"Is everything okay, Dr. Reid?"

"Everything looks good. Ms. Tucker is approximately six weeks pregnant, and I estimate her due date will be around February twenty-second. However, babies can come a week earlier or later."

Calum listened intently as the doctor revealed he'd drawn blood and the results should be in before the end of the week. He then gave some basic advice on weight management and physical activity, along with cautioning her not to use hot tubs, steam rooms and saunas.

"She will have to go through prenatal screening tests during her first, second and third trimesters to rule out any abnormalities."

Lucy's fingernails bit into Calum's palm. "How often will you do these tests?"

"The receptionist will give you a packet with all of the information. I will see you once a month for the first six months, then twice a month during your seventh and eighth months, and then every week during your ninth month. Mr. Ramsey, I recommend you read everything in the packet, because Ms. Tucker will need you to do things she won't be able to do as she advances in her pregnancy."

Calum exchanged a glance with Lucy, noting the beginnings of a frown settling into her features. "I'll make certain she won't overdo it."

The doctor smiled. "That's what I like to hear." He turned back to Lucy. "The receptionist will also make an appointment for you to see the dietitian and nutritionist. We usually schedule them on the same day, and recommend a light meal in between both sessions. A prescription with a three-month supply of prenatal vitamins will be faxed to your local pharmacy for you to pick up later today."

Reaching across the desk, Calum shook the doctor's hand. "Thank you. We'll see you again next month." Cupping Lucy's elbow, he helped her stand. "Let's go, sweetheart. After we see the receptionist, I'll take you to get something to eat."

Calum picked up the printed literature at the receptionist's desk and instructed the woman to make a copy of his credit card and to bill it for all of Lucy's medical and ancillary services. He'd like to put her on his insurance, but he knew that wasn't possible since she wasn't an employee or the spouse of an employee of Pins and Pints. Thankfully, she had her own insurance—but there were bound to be plenty of out-of-pocket costs. He'd make sure they came out of *his* pocket, not hers. He still had no idea how to be a parent, but at least he knew how to do this.

"I'd prefer to eat in Spring Forest," Lucy told Calum after he'd mentioned going to a restaurant in Raleigh once they left the doctor's office and were settled in his SUV.

"Do you think you can wait that long to eat?"

"Yes."

"Why don't you take a nap," he suggested. "I'll wake you once we get there."

"Oh-kay," she said with a yawn and closed her eyes.

When she'd revealed feeling fatigued, Dr. Reid had recommended she take naps throughout the day. Might as well start now. She felt weighed down with fatigue, and she believed part of it was from the shock of finally having her pregnancy definitively confirmed. It hadn't become a reality until a test in the doctor's office made it indisputable.

"This is why it makes sense for me to come to all the appointments," Calum stated. "That way, you can rest on the trip back."

Lucy opened her eyes. "You plan to go with me to all the appointments?"

Calum took a quick glance at her before returning his attention to the road. "Did you think my going with you today is a one-time occurrence?"

"I don't know, Calum. And truthfully, I know very little about you."

He smiled. "Well, we have another eight months to get to know each other. I'm in favor of spending as much time together as we can."

"I don't know if that's possible. We both have businesses to run."

"Why are you putting up roadblocks when there shouldn't be any? You have two assistants who are very capable of running Chapter One whenever you must step away. And now that you plan to close Sundays and Mondays during the summer, you'll have even more time for yourself."

Lucy knew Calum was right. She was fortunate to have Miss Grace and Ms. Fowler. Chapter One was doing well; Buttercup had a litter of five healthy puppies. Everything should have been on track—but then this pregnancy had thrown it all up in the air.

Her life plan did not include becoming a mother—at least for a few years. And more importantly, she wasn't sure what kind of ongoing relationship she'd have with Calum after having his child. They'd been friends for a year, yes, but they hadn't dated for long at all before becoming pregnant. Her parents had dated for more than seven months before discovering they were to become parents.

"Ms. Fowler and Miss Grace are retired, and I don't believe they'd want to work more than five hours a day, three days a week each."

"You won't know that unless you ask them. You're going to have to level with your employees and let them know you're pregnant and will have to take time off for doctor visits."

Lucy wanted to tell Calum that it was easy for him to say because she was the one carrying the baby, the one who would have to take more time off for maternity leave. "If they're not willing to increase their hours, then I'll have to hire a full-timer."

Calum rested his right hand on her knee. "I want you to know one thing, bae."

"What's that?"

"You're not alone. I'm going to be with you for the duration."

His touch was as reassuring at his pronouncement and Lucy knew she had to learn to trust Calum. Believe he would be there for her and their child.

Trouble was, that was easier said than done.

It was lunchtime at the Main Street Grille and Calum managed to get the last empty booth along a side wall. "What do you feel like eating?" he asked Lucy as she studied the menu.

Her head popped up and he went completely still. Calum found himself transfixed as he stared at Lucy. It was as if he was seeing her for the first time. Even without makeup, her bare face literally glowed with good health. Lucy Tucker wasn't just pretty. She was beautiful.

"How are the burgers?"

"Excellent. You've never ordered one?"

Lucy shook her head, soft waves moving around her face. "No. The few times I've eaten here, I've ordered a sandwich. But I'm really in the mood for a burger today."

"I always order the burgers because they're made with Angus beef."

"I'll also have a burger." Lucy reached for his

hand and increased the pressure on his fingers. "Can you have someone bring me a glass of water?"

Calum's brow furrowed. "Are you all right?"

Lucy leaned back against the booth at the same time she closed her eyes. Then, without warning, she sprang up, covered her mouth with her hand and headed in the direction of the restrooms. Calum was on his feet in seconds, running after her. He stood outside the ladies' room, wanting to go in, then changed his mind when he saw people staring at him.

He knocked on the door. "Lucy, are you all right?"

"Don't come in," ordered a woman's voice. "She'll be out soon."

Calum ran a hand over his face. A feeling of utter helplessness swept over him as he sagged against the wall, waiting for her to emerge. The door finally opened and he straightened as she emerged. His heart turned over when he saw her eyes. They were red from what obviously had been violent retching.

The woman who had been in the bathroom with Lucy patted his arm. "I went through the same thing when I was pregnant." Though her words were kind and her tone sympathetic, she'd said it loud enough for everyone sitting in the rear of the restaurant to hear her.

Calum put his arm around Lucy's waist and led her back to their booth, as dozens of pairs of eyes followed them. It wouldn't take long before folks in

Spring Forest knew that Lucy Tucker was pregnant with Calum Ramsey's baby.

A waitress came over to the table and set down a tall glass with a thick, milky liquid and a straw. "It's a banana and vanilla yogurt smoothie. It did the trick for me when I was carrying my little ones. Drink up, sweetie. It will settle your stomach."

Lucy managed a weak smile. "Thank you." She picked up the straw and took a sip. "I feel better already."

"I don't think you should have the burger," Calum said. "It may be too greasy. Why don't you order something lighter?"

She shook her head. "I think I'm going to stick with the smoothie."

"Don't you want something else to eat?"

"This will do for now, Calum. I plan to go through the literature in the folder to find out what foods help to alleviate morning sickness. Or should I say afternoon sickness? All day sickness?"

"Did the doctor say how long you'll have it?"

"He claims it usually ends after the first trimester. Hopefully I'll wake up one day and never experience it again before I reach three months."

All of this was new to Calum. His sister had been living on base with her army husband when she'd gotten pregnant. Calum hadn't been there to witness any of it.

"Will my ordering a burger bother you?"

"Of course not. I have to say this smoothie is delicious—and it's sitting very easily on my stomach. I have fruit, yogurt and almond milk at home. I can substitute the smoothie for a snack in between my meals."

"You can give me a list of foods that you need, and I'll get them ordered for you. I have an online account with the grocery store, and I usually have my groceries delivered with the kitchen orders to save me from having to go to the store. It's no trouble to add things for you, too. And after you read the pamphlets, let me know what you shouldn't eat so I'll exclude them whenever I make lunch for you. Is there anything else you need?"

"Not that I can think of. Oh, but you reminded me—now that the puppies' eyes are open, I've decided to bring them to the store. I need to order a large wire crate for them."

"You're going to tote the puppies back and forth every day?"

"Why not? They are small enough to fit in a laundry basket."

Calum clamped his jaw shut rather than tell Lucy that she was doing too much. She was taking care of a lactating dog with five puppies, running a bookstore, all while in the first stage of pregnancy. But he knew she wouldn't appreciate him pointing that out or implying that she couldn't handle it.

Instead, he decided to ask another question—one

that had just become quite pressing. "Are you ready for the gossip about me getting you pregnant, Lucy?"

Lucy took another sip of the delicious cold smoothie. "I'm not concerned about gossip, Calum." She had been a year ago, when she'd left Charlotte. But she'd done a lot of growing since then. And she wasn't going to let gossip chase her away this time. She gave him a direct look. "Are *you* ready?"

A beat passed. "I'm more than ready."

He hadn't seemed ready at all when they'd first talked about why he hadn't settled down—but she supposed the baby changed things for him. It certainly changed things for her. Lucy realized she didn't have the luxury of procrastinating about her impending motherhood. The baby was coming, whether she was ready or not.

"You never told me why you decided to settle here," Calum said in a quiet voice.

"I'll tell you later."

"I'm off tomorrow night. Would you mind if I come by?"

"I wouldn't mind at all. I'll make dinner."

"No, bae. I'll bring dinner."

Lucy smiled. "What if we cook together?"

Calum rested a hand over her flat belly. "Have you forgotten what happened the last time we cooked together?"

She placed her hand over his. "I will never forget

it, Calum. I…" Her words trailed when the waitress returned to the table to take their orders. Lucy ordered a fruit cup and Calum his medium-well burger with an iced tea.

They finished their lunch; he settled the check. Lucy thanked him and walked to Chapter One, while Calum headed for Pins and Pints. The bell chimed when she opened the door and she found Ms. Fowler sitting in the bookstore's reading area.

"I thought you'd finished that novel?"

Angela Fowler picked up a bookmark, slipped it between the pages and closed the book. "I did. But I never get tired of reading Jane Austen. How was your doctor's appointment?"

"Good. The doctor confirmed what I'd suspected. I'm pregnant."

Ms. Fowler pressed her palms together, applauding as fine smile lines fanned out around her brilliant blue eyes. "Oh, how wonderful. You and Calum will have a gorgeous child. I know there may come a time when you may need to take a few days off, and I'm willing to fill in any way I can."

"Thank you, Ms. Fowler."

"There's no need to thank me, Lucy. You know I love working here. And I'm also certain Evelyn will put in extra hours if you need her."

"We'll discuss that on Thursday before the read aloud. Oh, and just so you know, I'm planning to bring Buttercup and her puppies in every day—that way, I won't have to go home and walk her like I have been." The feeder system meant Lucy didn't have to worry about Buttercup running out of food during the day, but all the extra eating and drinking Buttercup was doing meant she needed more walks. "I've ordered an extra-large crate and freestanding pet gate to keep them from wandering around."

"Has she changed since she had her litter? I remember her growling every time I went into the office."

Lucy laughed softly. "She's very calm and easy-going these days. I'm going to go home to walk her right now, unless there's something you need me to take care of first?"

"Everything's fine here. Don't rush, Lucy. It's been kind of slow today. Maybe it will pick up later."

The bell chimed and Calum walked in, holding the folder containing her prenatal information.

"You left this in my car," he said, handing her the folder when she met him at the front.

"Thank you. I was just leaving to go home and take care of Buttercup."

Calum took her hand. "I'll walk you to your car."

Walking alongside Calum, with him holding her hand, wasn't anything new. What was new for Lucy was feeling protected. Her father had never protected her from his overbearing, overcritical mother, and Johnny was too egotistical to think of anyone but himself.

Lucy always thought of herself as a strong, in-dependent, free-thinking woman who didn't need anyone's protection—but she couldn't deny that it was nice to have it.

Her feelings for Calum were changing every day like the changes going on inside her body. She'd de-veloped a mutual respect for him as a fellow busi-ness owner right from the start. Before long, those feelings segued into an easygoing friendship. Some-where along the way, things changed and she began to see him as a man—a very attractive man. At-tractive enough, she'd begun to entertain romantic notions. Then came the sexual encounter that had changed them and their lives forever.

Lucy knew she had to put on her big girl panties and deal with the hand that had been dealt her. She didn't want to become too dependent on Calum's support when she wasn't sure he'd stand by her long term—but she didn't want to turn down any help she could get, either. When they reached her car in the parking lot, Calum let go of her hand to cradle her face between his palms.

"Drive carefully," he whispered as his head low-ered and he brushed a light kiss over her parted lips.

Lucy smiled. "I will. Thank you for going with me this morning."

Calum pressed the pad of his thumb to her lower lip. "What did I say about you thanking me? Everything I do for you is because I want to, Lucy. I don't want you to ever forget that."

She stared up at him through her lashes. "I'll try and remember that."

He gave a playful pat on her backside. "Go home and take care of Buttercup. Let her know that I'm coming to see her and her babies tomorrow."

"I will."

Lucy drove out of the lot, taking furtive glances at the rearview mirror to find Calum standing in the same spot where she'd left him. She was still thinking about him as she drove to Kingdom Creek and pulled into the driveway of her house.

When she let herself in, Buttercup stood up and shook herself. All the puppies were asleep, except Beignet. Last born and smallest of the litter, the little pup had caught up and surpassed her heavier brothers and sister. When feeding, she was first to latch on to a teat and the last to let go.

"Come, Buttercup. I'm going to take you for a walk so you can get some fresh air." Beignet squealed when she realized her mother was leaving her. "Sorry, sweetness," Lucy crooned to the puppy. "Your momma needs a break from you."

Beignet's crying woke the others and soon there was a cacophony of whines and squeals. Lucy ignored the puppies as she put on Buttercup's harness and lead, gathered a supply of poop bags and headed out the door.

The golden retriever appeared to enjoy being outdoors as she walked, stopping to sniff the grass and around fire hydrants. Twenty minutes later, Lucy returned to the house. After gulping down some water, Buttercup followed her into the living room, nudging her with her nose. "I know what you want," Lucy told the dog as she sank down to the floor. It had been a while since the dog had wanted to climb onto her lap and be held.

She gently stroked the head on her chest. "A lot of things have happened since you last let me hold you, little mama. You had your babies and now I'm going to have a baby, too. It only took you two months before you were ready to have your litter, while it's going to be nine months for me. I'm hoping to have one baby when compared to your five, but there may be a possibility of a multiple birth because Calum's sister has a set of twins." Buttercup looked as if she understood what Lucy was saying.

"Unlike you, I will get to keep my baby. But don't worry, honey. As soon as yours are weaned, they will go to their forever homes. I wish I could adopt you, but that's not going to be possible. Whoever does adopt you will get the sweetest dog in the world." Lucy kissed the top of the golden retriever's head. "I love you, baby girl." She laughed when Buttercup let out a low woof. "Yes, I know. You love me, too." When the cuddling session was over, she led Buttercup back to her puppies.

Lucy washed her hands in the half-bath before opening the refrigerator to look for a good snack option. She decided to take out a one-portion bag of washed salad greens and quickly added sliced chicken, avocado and mango. Normally, she would've added minced red onion but opted to leave it out until she read the pamphlet outlining what and what not to eat during pregnancy. She mixed the ingredients with a light olive oil and lime juice, ate slowly and drank a full glass of water. The salad would give her the energy she needed to power through the afternoon.

She'd begun her teaching career preparing lesson plans for her students and now, as a mother-to-be, she had to plan her meals not only to sustain her energy but to give her baby the best start in life via good nutrition.

Lucy returned to Chapter One and began the task of designing the window for the upcoming month. She'd decided to attach a banner with black-and-white piano keys across the window. Each white key would be stamped with holidays for the month: Juneteenth, World Blood Donor Day, National Camera Day, National Egg, World Bicycle, Cheese and Donut Days. She also included National Ice Cream Day, Take Your Dog to Work Day, World Music Day and International Day of the Tropics. She'd set out books that corresponded to the days and she hoped to see a small crowd gathered in front of her windows to stare at the colorful display.

It felt good to have everything organized and laid out. If only she could sort through her life that easily. But just as with the piano keys, all she could do was take it one thing at a time.

Chapter Eleven

Chapter One was buzzing with excitement when word circulated that Buttercup and her puppies were on the premises. And though the talk was less open, more whispered, there was even buzz when news spread throughout Spring Forest that the owner of the bookstore was pregnant, and the father was no other than Calum Ramsey.

He'd decided to ignore it all. Impending fatherhood was something he still was processing and, with each passing day, it became more difficult— not because it was demanding too much from him but because Lucy wouldn't permit him to do enough.

His concern was that she was burning the proverbial candle at both ends. She was working just as many hours as usual while also devoting every spare minute to Buttercup and her puppies. She never seemed to make time to rest, even on the day when he'd walked in to find her sitting in one of the chairs in the reading section as if she was trying to catch her breath. When he opened his mouth to say something, she'd immediately put up her hand to stop him. And then quietly asked him to leave because she was busy. He'd walked out, cursing under his breath, and taken a stroll around The Corners, a small strip of stores off Main Street, to calm down.

There came a light knock on the office door. "Yes!" The door opened and Aiden walked in. "You're in early." It was after one and Aiden was scheduled to work the six-to-eleven shift.

"I thought I'd come in early and hear it from the horse's mouth."

Tenting his fingers, Calum leaned back in his chair. "And what's that?"

"That you're going to become a papa. I was over at the Grille eating lunch and I overheard a couple talk about you and Lucy Tucker having a baby. Is it true?"

Light brown eyes met and locked with a pair of aquamarine blue. "Yes, it's true." Did Aiden expect him to deny it?

Aiden sank down to the chair in front of the desk and ran fingers through thick blond waves. "I always thought I'd become a father before you, Ramsey.

Especially with all of your talk about not wanting children."

"I never said I didn't want children," he countered defensively. "I said I wasn't ready."

Pale eyebrows lifted a fraction. "I suppose you're going to have to get ready."

"I don't have to do anything of the sort, Aiden. I already am ready."

Aiden smiled. "Good for you. And congratulations."

Calum also smiled. "Thanks."

"When's the wedding?"

Calum's smile slowly faded. He'd spent countless hours thinking of how he could bring up the topic of marriage with Lucy. He'd asked himself over and over if he loved Lucy enough to make that kind of commitment, and each time the answer was that he didn't know. What frightened him was that she was so easy to love. There was something about Lucy Tucker that had softened his heart to believe in love.

"We haven't discussed marriage." He hadn't broached the topic because more of Lucy's words were branded on his brain. *Regardless of whether we stay together, I want our son or daughter to know they're loved.* She was clearly prepared to raise their child as a single mother.

"I suppose you guys have time for that."

"That, we do."

Aiden rose to stand. "I'm out. I'll be back before you leave."

Calum waited for Aiden to leave to swivel in the chair and stare out the window overlooking the parking lot. There came another knock on the door and Calum got up to open it. He saw Timmy holding the bag with Lucy's lunch. "What is it?"

"Miss Grace said Miss Lucy went out and told her she didn't need lunch today."

"Thank you, Timmy. Please put it in the fridge."

Calum massaged his forehead with his fingertips, wondering where Lucy could've gone to eat. They had established a habit of talking to each other at least once a day. She called him once she arrived at the bookstore, and he called her whenever he began his night shift. However, he found it odd that today she hadn't contacted him. He decided that, later on, he'd have to visit the bookstore.

Lucy entered the bookstore through the rear door and was met with a welcoming bark from Buttercup. "Hey," she whispered. "You're going to wake up your babies." The puppies were sprawled over one another on the mattress in the extra-large crate. They all were gaining weight and looked like little round balls of fur. She opened a drawer in the workstation, stored her cross-body, and slipped on a smock.

She'd driven to Raleigh for a group session with the nutritionist and dietitian. The information she'd gleaned from both would be invaluable when planning meals. She and four other women were offered a nutritious lunch with lean meat, steamed vegetables, and roasted potatoes, sliced bananas and applesauce, along with fruit-flavored carbonated water and ginger ale with real ginger to offset morning sickness.

Buttercup returned to the crate as Lucy left the office, closing the door behind her. She noticed the members of a local book club gathering in the reading area. They'd agreed to purchase all their titles from Chapter One with the proviso they could use the store for their meeting place.

She picked up several paperbacks, left on a side table, that needed to be reshelved. The bell chimed as the door opened and Calum walked in. He looked good in a white shirt, unbuttoned at the neck, cuffs rolled back to display strong wrists, and a pair of slim-cut jeans and shiny black low-heeled boots—and she wasn't the only one to notice. Several of the book club women were staring at him.

Lucy tried to avoid doing the same. She had consciously avoided him for several days because she needed to be alone with her thoughts and work through her feelings. And yet despite the time she'd taken, she was still uncertain whether she loved Calum enough to spend the rest of her life with him. There was still so much about him she felt she didn't know. Especially when it came to his father. He was reluctant to talk about the man, except to say he hadn't been around much. As his friend, Lucy had never felt it was her place to pry. But as the woman who would be raising a child with him, his experiences with his father felt like something she needed to understand.

Calum approached her, cupping her elbow. "Why didn't you tell me you were going back to the doctor?"

Lucy was taken aback. "Say what?"

"Why did I have to hear from someone else that you were in Raleigh today? Don't I have the right to know if something happened with the baby? How could you keep that from me?"

Lucy drew herself up to her full height. "It's clear you're upset," she said crisply. "You should go. Come back when you've calmed down enough to talk to me instead of interrogating me."

He clenched his jaw then dropped his hand. "We'll talk about this later."

Lucy watched as he exited. She turned to see everyone in the store staring at her. It was apparent they'd witnessed the tense interchange. "I'm sorry about that," she said, apologizing to her customers.

"There's no need to apologize," crooned one of the book club members. "You'll probably kiss and make up before the night is over."

Lucy wanted to tell her that wasn't going to happen. Not after he'd stormed in and made a scene, embarrassing her in front of people she relied on to keep the doors to Chapter One open.

She'd told Calum she really didn't know him, and he'd proved her right.

"Here, Lucy. I think you could use some water."

She smiled at Miss Grace who had filled a paper cup with water from the office's watercooler. "Thank you."

"Are you sure you're all right?"

She took a sip of the cool liquid, staring at her assistant over the rim. "I am now," she said truthfully.

A frown settled into Evelyn Grace's features. The petite middle-aged woman with dark brown smiling eyes wrung her hands. "Even though I think of Calum as one of Spring Forest's finest young men, it was wrong of him to come at you like he'd caught you doing something wrong."

Lucy couldn't stop the smile parting her lips at the woman's support.

"Not to worry, Miss Grace. That will not happen again."

Evelyn Grace made a sucking sound with her tongue and teeth. "It better not or he'll definitely get a mouthful from me."

Lucy took another sip, pondering the situation she was now in. It had taken a week before all of Spring Forest had become aware of her pregnancy, and she knew it would take even less for what had just occurred to become fodder for the town's rumor mill.

The Lucy of a year ago would have started looking for options to head to someplace new. But that wasn't her anymore. No more running away. No more concerning herself with what people thought of her. She was Lucy Rebecca Tucker, former schoolteacher, resident of Spring Forest, North Carolina, bookstore owner, foster of a golden retriever with a litter of five, and pregnant. She wasn't going anywhere, wasn't going to give up all she'd built over the past year. She wanted to set a good example for her baby, and that meant standing her ground.

"I'll be back as soon as I walk Buttercup," she informed Miss Grace. Walking the dog was the antidote for her to clear her head. She always felt better after walking or having a monologue with the gentle canine.

Calum knew he'd messed up. Big-time! He didn't know what had possessed him to go into Chapter One and disrespect Lucy the way he had. Within seconds of walking out of the bookstore, he'd realized his boorish behavior bordered on bullying.

He'd grown up in a household with women—mother, grandmother and sister—and he'd gotten an earful from both his mother and grandmother once he'd begun dating. Their message that followed him into adulthood: *if you don't respect the woman you're with, you obviously don't deserve her.* And he had disrespected Lucy in her place of business and in the presence of her customers. Judging by their disapproving looks, he didn't deserve her.

"I think you need to drink something stronger than that fizzy water you're staring at, boss."

Calum's head popped up and he looked at Jake.

"Nah, Jake. I'm good."

Jake rested both elbows on the bar and leaned closer. "You haven't been good since you had that dustup with Lucy Tucker."

"You know about that?"

"You can't be that obtuse, boss," he said in a quiet voice. "Practically everyone in Spring Forest knows. After all, this isn't Raleigh or even Charlotte. Out here, gossip spreads faster than a lighted fuse attached to a stick of dynamite. Some folks are calling it a lover's spat, while others are saying not so nice things about you. And if you hadn't been so involved in your own pity party, you'd have noticed even some of the workers giving you the stink eye. Particularly your female employees."

Calum cursed under his breath. Jake was right. He'd been wallowing in self-pity when what he needed to do was man up and apologize to Lucy. He was even ready to grovel if it meant not losing her. Reaching in the pocket of his jeans, he took out his cell phone and scrolled through the apps until he found the one he wanted. It took less than ten minutes to decide on a peace offering.

"You really like this woman, don't you?" Jake asked as Calum put away the smartphone.

"You think I shouldn't?"

Jake stood straight. "I know it's not about the baby, boss. She had you twisted in knots the first day she walked in here and introduced herself." He held up a hand to stop Calum when he opened his mouth. "Please let me finish. The expression on your face reminded me of that line from *Casablanca* when Ingrid Bergman walks into Humphrey Bogart's bar. Instead of 'gin joints,' it was, of all the bowling alleys in all the towns in all the world, she walks into mine."

Throwing back his head, Calum laughed. "You definitely watch too many movies." Jake had admitted he had a collection of nearly three hundred movies, many of them in black-and-white. "If I remember correctly, the Bogart character didn't end up with the girl."

"That's right. Is that what you want?" Jake asked, crossing heavily tattooed arms over his chest. "Are you willing to risk losing the girl and your baby?"

Calum sobered, his expression a mask of stone. "No, Jake. That's not going to happen. Not in this lifetime." Even if he and Lucy couldn't make a go of it with each other, there was no way he would abandon his child like his father did. "I'm not going to lose Lucy or the baby."

Because it wasn't only about the baby she was carrying but also Lucy herself. Calum had been waging a private war with his emotions for more than a year, trying not to fall for her. He'd not only lost the battle but also the war.

His bartender was right on point when he talked about his reaction to meeting Lucy. He still remembered what she'd been wearing: a white silk man-tailored shirt, a pair of black, cropped linen-gabardine slacks and matching ballet slippers. Her wavy bob had been held off her face with a headband covered with a black-and-white African mud cloth print. Calum had been stunned by her casual look that showcased such understated sophistication. Her beautiful face and low, smoky voice had held him captive until something in his brain jolted him into enough awareness to introduce himself.

"That's what I want to hear," Jake drawled, smiling. "You probably don't want me to talk about your lady. But the night she walked in here wearing that sexy-ass dress, I was ready to jump over the bar and ask her out myself. But then, when she called you 'darling,' I decided it wasn't worth the effort to embarrass myself."

Calum looked at Jake as if he'd taken leave of his senses. "You were thinking about hitting on my woman when you have one?"

Jake reached for a glass and filled it with ginger ale. "Lisa and I have called it quits—for good this time. We've split up so many times that we decided it's better if we don't see each other for a while. She's set in her ways, and I can be stubborn as a mule, and there're times when we just can't compromise."

Calum nodded. He knew a lot about the inability to compromise. His parents had never been able to agree—on anything. It wasn't what he wanted for himself and Lucy.

Picking up the glass with club soda, he drained it and then set it on the bar. "Thanks for the pep talk. You can send me your bill."

"You can't afford me, boss."

He gave Jake a fist bump. "You're right about that." He liked talking to the bartender because Jake was objective and unapologetic.

But on the subject of apologies…he knew he owed one to Lucy. He was just so insecure about how to be a good father that the smallest thing could make him overreact and lash out. It was an ongoing struggle to trust himself that he could become a good father—especially when he wasn't sure whether she would be willing to allow him to share her life. She'd talked about raising their child as a single mother, making it clear that she had no problem excluding him from his child's life if it came to that. Well, he had no intention of that happening. Not while there was breath in his body.

He'd known the emptiness of not having his father around when growing up, and that wasn't something he wanted for his son or daughter. He wanted his baby to grow up strong and confident, able to love freely and openly in all the ways that Calum still struggled with.

Calum didn't know what it was about Lucy Tucker that had, as Jake put it, twisted him into knots and kept him from a restful night's sleep. Some people talked about someone being their soul mate, and he wondered if she was his. Only time would tell, and he had months before Lucy was expected to give birth; hopefully, he would be able to find the missing piece in the puzzle of his life to make it a complete picture.

Lucy had called Furever Paws to let them know she was bringing knitted garments for the upcoming puppy and kitten shower so that someone could meet her in the parking lot to carry the storage bins. She'd become very careful when it came to lifting anything weighing more than a couple of pounds. The heaviest thing she'd handled lately had been the enormous fruit and flower basket that had been delivered to the bookstore that morning. The card attached to the basket contained a single word: Sorry!

He was sorry and Lucy missed him. Even though she'd talked about how she could handle being a single mother if the situation called for it, she didn't want to raise their child alone. She'd grown up with an absentee father who'd thought sending checks would fulfill his responsibility of being a father.

Lucy knew it was time for them to have a face-to-face and air their differences. And she was going to stand firm—that she would not allow him to treat her with disrespect.

One of the male volunteers came out to the parking lot and effortlessly carried the storage bins. Lucy closed the SUV's hatch and thanked him, telling him how much she was looking forward to the fashion show. Goodness knew, the shelter could use a windfall, especially with the additional costs it had taken on to house and care for all those poor animals from the backyard breeder. It was great to hear that the local philanthropist, Regina Mackenzie, had agreed to host the puppy and kitten fundraiser to raise money for the shelter.

Although she'd wanted to stay and chat with the volunteer, Lucy knew it was time to return to the bookstore. Before pulling out of the parking lot, she activated the Bluetooth device and tapped the screen when Calum's private number appeared. It rang twice before he answered.

"Hello."

She paused. His greeting was low and breathless. "Did I wake you?" Lucy had forgotten he alternated working the night shift with his assistant manager, leading to an unusual sleep schedule.

"No," he said quickly.

"Why do you sound so breathless?"

"I just finished jogging on the treadmill."

"I can call you back once you catch your breath."

"No! Please don't. I'm good now."

Lucy adjusted the air-cooling system to maximum to offset the brutal rays of the sun coming through the windshield. "You should be careful not to overdo it. I don't want our baby to grow up without its father."

"We need to talk, Lucy."

She nodded even though he couldn't see her. "I know."

"I'd like you, Buttercup and the puppies to spend weekends at my place. The more time we spend together, the better we'll get to know each other."

Lucy hadn't known what to expect but it wasn't Calum inviting her to spend time at his house. "Okay," she said quickly, before she could make up an excuse to turn him down. "But aren't you working weekends?"

"I've worked out an agreement with Aiden to take time off for family matters and he's agreed to fill in whenever I need him."

"Does Aiden know that you're going to become a father?"

A low laugh came through the earpiece. "Yes."

"Did you tell him, Calum?"

"No. He heard it through the Grille's grapevine."

She rolled her eyes upward. "Is it at all possible to keep a secret in Spring Forest?"

Calum laughed again. "I don't think so. I know you don't close on Saturday until six, so I'll come by your house sometime after seven to get you and the dogs. And, Lucy, don't bother to pack up any doggie stuff. I'll make sure to have everything they'll need. Buttercup and the pups can have the run of the patio."

"I'm planning to take them to the fundraiser at Furever Paws. It's coming up soon, you know. I just dropped off my donations."

"I'll come with you, Lucy," Calum volunteered, "because there's no way you'll be able to manage six dogs by yourself. The puppies alone are a handful."

"They are," she admitted. "Everyone knows when they're in the bookstore because of the continual barking and yelping. My puppy daughters are the biggest troublemakers. Whenever Buttercup and the rest of the litter attempt to sleep, Pancake and Beignet begin wrestling with each other and soon there's a puppy MMA cage match."

"What about when they're home with you?"

"It doesn't matter where they are. A few times, they woke me up."

"That's not good, Lucy. You need your sleep."

"I take power naps in the back during the day, and I go to bed earlier than I used to."

"No more sitting up reading or watching movies?" Calum teased.

"Movies and reading are on hold. Now that I'm in the knitting mood, thanks to the work I've done for the fundraiser, I've ordered yarn to make hats, sweaters and booties for baby Tucker-Ramsey." Lucy shifted into gear and drove out of the lot.

"Tucker-Ramsey, Lucy? You want to hyphenate the baby's last name?"

She waited at an intersection before maneuvering into the flow of traffic. "Yes. I want our child to grow up knowing where they've come from if they ever want to do their genealogy."

"No comment."

Lucy got the sense that Calum was conflicted when it came to his father, but that was something he would have to work through on his own journey to becoming a father.

"I want to thank you for the flowers and the fruit basket. It was very thoughtful of you to send them."

"It was the only thing I could think of to get out of the clichéd doghouse."

"You're out. Just try and stay out."

"Yes, ma'am. I'll come over before you close to help you load up your SUV with everything."

"Thank you."

"Later, Calum."

"Later, bae."

Lucy disconnected the call. She also knew she and Calum had reached a point in their relationship that needed to be resolved. And, hopefully, some of her uncertainty about their future would be put to rest during the weekends they would spend together.

Chapter Twelve

Lucy would have been the first one to admit that she was overwhelmed. Running the bookstore and taking care of five puppies had begun to take its toll. It was all she could do to make it through the day without falling asleep whenever she sat down.

She was still experiencing morning sickness, but not just in the morning. It occurred at any time of the day and could be triggered by something she'd eaten or smelled. She'd changed her perfume to one with lighter notes, and she'd delayed eating breakfast until after she arrived at the bookstore. Yet the nausea continued to pop up at the most inopportune times. She'd gotten in the habit of keeping a toothbrush, paste and mouthwash on hand at all times.

Her employees had become her fairy godmothers, coming in earlier and staying later so that she'd be able to take a minute for herself whenever she needed it. Ms. Fowler had taken over as moderator of the Teddy Bear Storytime on Thursday evenings and soon wowed the kids with her voices for different characters. What had begun with six attendees had swelled to an average of twelve, ranging in age from three to eight. Ms. Fowler alternated reading two books for the preschoolers and one chapter book for the older children.

It was a relief to know that the story time was in good hands, but she still had a pile of responsibilities. To the store. To her customers. To her baby. To Buttercup. Even to Calum. Since he wanted to be involved as a father, she owed it to him to find a way to make that work. She'd convinced herself his concern was for the baby and not its mother. The practical side of Lucy Tucker acknowledged there wouldn't be declarations of love because they were casual friends who had slept together once and it had resulted in a pregnancy. But the unrealistic Lucy wanted Calum to love her *and* the baby growing beneath her heart. She and the baby were a package deal and she needed him to want both.

Lucy was aware that he was a very eligible bachelor and had heard rumors that a few women were interested in him. Had his interest in her come from her appearing immune to his obvious good looks and success as one of Spring Forest's new and young entrepreneurs? Had she become a challenge he'd found impossible to ignore? Or did he genuinely like her? That was probably a question she should have asked *before* sleeping with him. Now that a baby was in the picture, they didn't really have the option to try out being together and then decide whether or not it worked. For better or for worse, there was something permanent connecting them now, and they needed to figure out how to deal with that.

Lucy hoped, after spending several weekends with Calum, they would finally have a plan to move forward.

"There you go, little mama." Calum set Buttercup on the ground but not before Buttercup pressed her wet nose to his face. Smiling, he lifted the crate with the five rambunctious puppies barking and whining to escape their wire enclosure.

Calum knew asking Lucy to spend the weekends with him was wholly selfish on his part. He really did think they should get to know each other better before the baby was born. But he also wanted to use this time to make certain of what he felt and was beginning to feel for this woman. He loved her, which was a new feeling for him. He needed some time to get used to it.

No other woman he'd dated even came close to Lucy. They'd tried too hard to say and do things they'd believed he liked or wanted, where Lucy said exactly what was on her mind. He admired her forthrightness and the way she unknowingly made him rethink what he wanted for his future.

Knowing that he wanted her was the easy part. What was harder was figuring out what he had to offer in return. His greatest fear was not being a good husband and father. Keith Ramsey may have had the best intentions, but in the end, he was either unable or unwilling to overcome his weaknesses of character. Lucy deserved a partner as strong and capable as she was. Calum needed to figure out if he could be that man.

Calum handed Lucy the keys to the front door. "I'll bring everything in."

"I can carry my bags."

"It's okay, Lucy. I've got this." Dipping his head, Calum kissed her cheek. "Go inside and rest." He'd noticed during the drive from her house that her eyelids were drooping. "After I get Biscuit, Bagel, Bialy, Brioche and Blintz settled, I'll fix dinner for us."

Lucy cut her eyes at him. "You know right well that's not their names."

He wiggled his eyebrows. "I just happen to like alliterations like Pins and Pints."

"If you like alliterations so much, do you plan to name your son Robert Royce Tucker-Ramsey, or your daughter Ramona Ruth Tucker-Ramsey?"

Calum shook his head. "No, bae. Once we find

out if we're having a boy or girl, we'll decide together on a name."

"You want to know the sex of the baby before it's
born?" Lucy asked.

"Yes. Why?"

"I just thought you'd want to be surprised."

"I was surprised when you told me I was going
to be a father. I don't need any more for a while."
Calum saw an expression cross Lucy's face. "You
don't want to know." His question was a statement.

"I haven't made up my mind. I ordered yarn in
varying shades of yellow and green so I can make
things that are gender neutral. Personally, I don't like
colors assigned to specific genders."

"Maybe you'll have twins like my sister. One of
each."

"Oh no! No, no, Calum. Don't even open your
mouth to say something like that."

He grimaced when she turned on her heel and
stomped toward the front door. It was obvious he'd
said the wrong thing, though he wasn't sure exactly
where he'd misstepped. Kayla had always wanted two
children—a boy and a girl—and when she'd had the
twins, she'd stated that her family was complete. What
did Lucy picture when she thought of a full, complete
family? He didn't know, but he wanted to find out.

Solar lights had illuminated the rear of the house
as dusk descended on Spring Forest. Lucy shifted

into a more comfortable position on the patio recliner as she watched the puppies explore the extra-large, waterproof outdoor kennel, while Buttercup lay on the ground next to Calum. When he'd mentioned he had doggie items, she hadn't suspected he would go all-out like this.

"It's like a doggie condominium."

Calum smiled at her over his shoulder. "I believe they really like it."

Lucy laughed as Beignet and Pancake chased each other around the patio. "It looks as if the girls can now burn off some of their energy and allow their mother and brothers to sleep undisturbed."

"They are truly in charge of everything."

The puppies were growing up so quickly. Lucy knew it wouldn't be long before they were completely weaned and eligible to be adopted. She'd mostly managed not to become too attached to the puppies because she knew she wouldn't have them long. However, it was different with Buttercup. She'd grown to love the beautiful golden retriever. As if summoned by her thoughts, Buttercup came over and climbed onto her lap.

Calum stood. "Do you think it's wise to let a fifty-pound dog lay on you?"

Lucy stroked Buttercup behind her ears. "Most of her weight is on my legs and thighs. You wouldn't hurt me, would you, baby girl?" she crooned. Buttercup pressed her head against Lucy's breasts, and she gritted her teeth. They were so sensitive to any pressure these days. The water from her shower felt like millions of pinpricks.

"Are you all right?"

She blew out a breath. "Yes."

Calum clapped his hands and Buttercup scrambled off Lucy's lap. "Come, Buttercup. We're going to go for a walk before you turn in for the night."

Lucy knew she hadn't convinced Calum that she was okay, and wondered if she would be able to get anything past him. "I'm going to stay here and keep an eye on the puppies."

Calum leaned over and kissed her. "Make certain they don't watch you dozing off, sleepyhead."

She swatted at him, but he was too fast and dodged her hand. "Don't forget that we have the puppy and kitten shower tomorrow."

He tapped his head. "I've already penciled it in."

"What, you wrote it down in your head? Are you telling me you are eidetic?"

Sitting at the foot of the recliner, Calum massaged her bare feet. "Yes. Having what folks call a photographic memory is one of the things that allowed me to graduate high school at sixteen and college two months before I turned twenty. It helped me pick things up faster than my classmates. I struggled every day not to blurt out the answers whenever my teachers asked questions. I had a geometry class where I wouldn't speak up and the teacher sent a note home to my mother asking to see her. I knew that would be problematic for Mom because she worked the two jobs, so I asked my grandmother to come instead."

Lucy was so intrigued by what Calum was telling her, that she hadn't realized she'd been holding her breath until she felt tightness in her chest. "What happened?"

"The teacher couldn't figure out how I was getting perfect test scores when I never participated in class. Honestly, she thought I was cheating, but she didn't know how I could be pulling it off."

"What did your grandmother tell her?"

Calum smiled, drawing her attention to his beautiful eyes, eyes she hoped her son or daughter would inherit.

"Nana didn't hold back when she asked her if she preferred a quiet student to one that cut the fool and disrupted her class. When my teacher didn't answer, Nana got up and warned her never to send home another note complaining about me behaving in class."

"I like your grandmother. Is she still alive?"

"Yes. And I can't wait for you to meet her. I know she'll love you because you're both feisty."

Lucy pushed out her lips. "I don't think of myself as feisty. In fact, I think I'm rather chill."

"Yeah, right," Calum drawled. He gave her toes a gentle squeeze. "Let's go, Buttercup. Your mama will watch your babies while we take a stroll around the neighborhood."

Lucy moved off the recliner because she knew if she'd stayed put, she probably would fall asleep. Bending slightly, she rubbed Fritter's back when he came over to sniff her feet. Although the puppies were nearly identical, she was always able to tell them apart. Grits and Beignet came over and soon she had three little wet tongues tasting her ankles and toes.

She sank down to the ground and within seconds bundles of fur were climbing all over her. "Like mama, like babies," she said, laughing. It was apparent they'd watched Buttercup climb onto her lap and reached the conclusion that it was the thing to do. Pancake and Waffle snuggled against her thigh and fell asleep.

Lucy lost track of time as she cuddled the puppies. She knew she was going to miss seeing them running and tumbling and wrestling with one another for the possession of a new toy. A rubber chicken had become a favorite and, within days, the chew toy was unrecognizable when used as a prop for tug-of-war.

Since their birth, the puppies' squeaking and whining had gradually been replaced by yelping and barking. Fritter was the first pup to discover he could bark longer and louder than his littermates and he used it to his advantage when establishing his authority as firstborn.

Lucy ran a forefinger down Fritter's back. "I know whoever adopts you will quickly learn that you are a natural leader." She shifted her attention to Pancake. "I really shouldn't say this, but you are my favorite among the litter. You get that little devilish look on your face just before you get into something you know you're not supposed to, and when you hook up with Beignet, you're like tag-team partners ready to take all comers. I know it's probably not possible, but I'd like for you and your sister to be adopted together." She paused, staring at the puppies pressed against her body. "I wish I could adopt you all, but that's not possible because my house is just too small for six dogs."

"It's not impossible."

Lucy's head popped up. Calum had returned without making a sound. "Where's Buttercup?"

He sat down next to her. "She's inside. I heard what you said about wanting to adopt all the dogs."

"That's just wishful thinking, Calum."

"It doesn't have to be if you marry me."

Fighting to hold back laughter, Lucy said, "I should marry you so I can have six dogs? You have to know that sounds as lame as me wanting to have six dogs in the first place." Calum's expression reminded her of someone being caught doing something they knew was wrong.

He dropped his head. "It does sound lame, but

you have to agree there's more than enough room in this house for Buttercup, her puppies *and* our baby."

Lucy extended her legs, disturbing two of the puppies. Grits turned around twice before settling down again. "I'll admit to that, but it's a moot point. You're acting like I should marry you just because I'm carrying your child, but that's not a good enough reason for me. I don't believe in repeating history."

Calum moved closer to Lucy until their shoulders were touching. "What aren't you saying?"

"My father was forced to marry my mother when she told him she was pregnant with his baby."

Calum just looked confused. "Forced? What are you talking about? You're not even thirty. No one was being forced to marry anyone thirty years ago. That kind of thing stopped happening ages ago."

"Maybe it's not as common as it used to be, but it still happens, especially with families like my father's. He'd been promised to marry another woman when he slept with my mother and got her pregnant."

Calum's gaze narrowed. "Promised or engaged?"

"I said 'promised,' Calum."

"Like an arranged marriage?" he asked.

Lucy wanted to laugh at his shocked expression, but what she had to tell him was no laughing matter. "I'm certain you're aware of bougie Black families. You know, the kind that grooms their children to attend elite HBCUs, pledge Divine Nine fraternities and sororities, become members of the Junior League and The Links and all that."

"I've met a few of those at Duke," Calum admitted. "But what does that have to do with your parents?"

"My mother wasn't any of *those*. She was the first in her family to attend and graduate college. But my dad's family had this whole lineage they were proud of. He could trace HBCU graduates in his family as far back as the beginning of the twentieth century. The girl he was dating was the daughter of one of his father's law partners. They weren't officially engaged, which allowed Adam Tucker the freedom to sleep around without technically cheating. But when my mother told him she was pregnant and keeping the baby, all hell broke loose."

Calum blinked slowly. "His family forced him to marry your mother to protect the family's name?"

"Bingo. No Tucker had ever had an *outside baby*. His mother insisted on the wedding—but then she accused my mom of trapping her son. That began a cold war between the two families with me as the pawn. Dad's mother insisted on paying for my music, dance and etiquette lessons so I would grow up to be a social granddame like all the women in her family.

"However, it was my mother's mother that had the greatest impact on my life. Grammie was an incredible homemaker and dressmaker, and she taught me to cook, knit and crochet. Once I learned to read, we would spend hours together reading to each other.

"My fondest memories were us cooking together. Sunday dinners were special in my home when we'd set the table with linen tablecloths, china, crystal and silver. The dinnerware was a wedding gift from Dad's mother, who said they should be used only for special occasions. The one time Grammie told her Sundays were special for us, she stopped coming to our house."

"So the mothers-in-law didn't get along."

"They were like oil and water. Grandmother never accepted my mother, and Grammie was always one step from cussing her out. She did tell Grandmother that she'd raised a weakling son who was afraid to make a move unless he checked in with Mommy Dearest."

Calum rested an arm over Lucy's shoulders. "How old were you when all of this went down?"

"I believe I was six when I became aware of it. I was about seven when my mother stopped going with Dad to his family's social gatherings, so it was just us. However, that ended when I overheard Grandmother tell one of her friends that my mother was a whore who got pregnant on purpose. When I told her she shouldn't say those nasty things about my mother, she said I was just as bad-mannered and ungrateful as my mother, and then said she never wanted to see me again."

"What did your father say?"

"Nothing. He claimed his mother had had a bad day. It also became his bad day when Mom said she wanted a divorce. I don't remember my father moving out, but one morning I got up and all of his clothes were gone."

"Good for her. And good for you, Lucy, for standing up for your mother in the first place. You were feisty even as a girl."

"If you say so."

"I say so, bae," Calum countered as he buried his face in her hair.

"I noticed the change in my mother immediately once her divorce was finalized. It was like a weight was off her shoulders, to finally be free of my dad's family and their judgment. I believe, deep down inside, that my father loved my mother, but he was too weak or intimidated by his mother to defy her.

"When he heard that Mom was going to marry again, he panicked and begged her to take him back, but she wasn't having it. She'd found a man that loved and respected her, and thankfully there was no interfering mother-in-law for either of them. His mother was dead, and my grammie passed away in her sleep my first year in college. There are times when I still grieve for her."

Calum's hand caressed her back. "Maybe if we have a girl, you can name her after your grammie."

"I don't think so, Calum. It's too similar to my name. Grammie's name was Lucinda."

His hand stilled. "What about a different variation, like Lucrezia?"

She shuddered noticeably. "Whenever I hear that name, I'm reminded of the Borgias and the rumors of incest, murder and poisoning. I have time to come up with names for our son or daughter." She paused. "Now you know the whole sordid story why I can't marry you just because I'm pregnant with your baby."

"What about love, Lucy?"

"What about it, Calum?"

"Would you marry me if you loved me? Baby or no baby?"

She thought about when she and Johnny had pledged their undying love for each other. It hadn't been enough for him, and that had damaged her ability to believe in undying love. "I don't know," she whispered.

"What's there not to know?" he asked.

"Love is fickle, Calum. People fall in and out of it. I can tell you that I love you today, and I just might change my mind next week. Love isn't the same as trust—it doesn't last the same way." Not that trust always lasted, either. She'd trusted her fiancé and he'd betrayed her.

"Do you trust me?" Calum asked her.

"I do. For now," she added. Lucy knew Calum

didn't like her answer when his expression changed, becoming a mask of stone.

"Is what we have a test for you, Lucy?"

"Are you questioning why I'm with you?" she asked him. "Because you should know it's not about this baby."

"What is it about?" he asked, his tone deceptively calm.

"It's about us, and only us."

Calum rose slightly and slanted his mouth over hers, deepening the kiss as moans erupted from the back of her throat. His free hand searched under her blouse and gently squeezed her breast. Her breath was coming faster and faster until Lucy felt dizzying currents of desire racing through her from head to toe. He stoked smoldering embers of longing that had refused to die out after their first encounter. His kisses and caresses reignited memories of the passion they'd shared the day they'd conceived their child.

A familiar sound penetrated the fog of desire threatening to swallow her whole. Lucy pulled back to see that it was Buttercup. She stood inside the doors leading to the patio, whining and barking.

"Calum, you need to let Buttercup out," Lucy whispered against his marauding mouth trailing kisses along the column of her neck.

He groaned. "To be continued."

"Yes. To be continued," she repeated. "I'm going

inside to shower, and then take care of Buttercup and the puppies before I call it a night."

Calum carefully removed the puppies off Lucy's lap, set them on their feet and then kissed her forehead. "Go to bed and sleep in as late as you want. I'll take care of the dogs."

"Are you sure?"

He kissed her again. "Doubly sure, bae."

Cradling his face in her palms, Lucy's mouth grazed his jaw. "Good night." He stood and, cupping her elbow, eased her to her feet. She walked to the patio doors and within seconds of opening them, Buttercup ran past her to reach her puppies.

It wasn't until she climbed the staircase to the second story that Lucy felt a wave of fatigue wash over her. She walked into the en suite guest bathroom and made quick work of brushing her teeth and showering before pulling on a nightgown.

When Calum unloaded her weekender bag from his SUV, he'd left it in the guest bedroom. He'd earned a point on Lucy's approval scale by not assuming they would share a bedroom. She appreciated the respect he was showing for her by making it clear that sleeping under his roof did not require her to share his bed.

Lucy lay in bed, closed her eyes and thought about Calum's impromptu marriage proposal. Had he proposed to test her? If she'd said yes, would he have been willing to follow through and marry her? She wasn't sure. She couldn't let go of a nagging fear that his proposal was all about the baby. After saying before that he wasn't looking for marriage and fatherhood, he'd done a complete one-eighty and now seemed to want both.

He could have both—but that was only possible if she allowed herself to trust again, and Lucy knew that was going to be very difficult for her. Once burned, twice shy.

Chapter Thirteen

The parking lot at Furever Paws was crowded with cars, pickups, vans and SUVs when Calum maneuvered into a space. He'd gotten up early to shower and let the dogs out, then returned to make breakfast. He'd wanted to surprise Lucy with breakfast in bed, but she'd come into the kitchen just as he'd placed a plate with grits, fluffy scrambled eggs and salmon cakes on a lap tray. She'd kissed him then apologized for spoiling his surprise, and suggested he warn her in advance next time so she'd know to stay put.

Lucy was the first woman, other than his mother, grandmother and sister, to sleep under his roof, and he wanted her to stay not just for weekends but for every day of the week. Lucy admitted she'd volunteered to foster Buttercup because she'd felt lonely. And if he were sincerely honest with himself, Calum had to acknowledge that he, too, was lonely. Even though he spent his days surrounded by other people, whenever he came home and closed the door, he was all alone.

He'd shared breakfast with women in the past, yet today it was different with Lucy. Sitting across from her in the breakfast nook, watching her eat and talk excitedly about the Furever Paws fundraiser, he couldn't help feeling charmed. She was so excited to show off Buttercup and her puppies, reminding him of a proud mama with her baby. It made him fantasize about what it would be like to sit with her in maybe a year's time, talking about plans she had for them to spend a lazy weekend day with their baby. He liked the thought of that.

It had taken Calum a while to accept that he was going to be a father. He'd spent a lot of time worrying about repeating history and making the same mistakes as his father, but there were some things he knew he could do right. He had the means to provide financial support for his son or daughter, which always helped, even if that wasn't enough on its own.

"It looks like a good turnout," he said, shutting off the engine.

Lucy unbuckled her belt. "Bunny and Birdie always keep their fingers crossed whenever there is a fundraising event," she said, referring to the elderly sisters who had founded Furever Paws years before. Although there was a director who ran operations these days, the sisters had stayed heavily involved in the shelter's operations. Bunny had been gone for a stretch recently—road-tripping with the boyfriend she'd met online. But she'd come back not that long ago and had stepped right into the swing of things again. "It's not easy for nonprofits to raise enough money to cover their expenses. This has been an especially rough year."

Calum met Lucy's eyes. She'd brushed her hair back from her face and styled it in a ponytail. She looked like a fresh-faced ingenue with her white man-tailored shirt, navy-blue leggings and white Converse sneakers. "Are you hinting that you want me to make a generous donation?"

A hint of a smile lifted the corners of Lucy's mouth. "I thought I was being subtle."

Undoing his seat belt, Calum leaned over and kissed her. "There's nothing about you that's ever subtle," he whispered against her parted lips.

Her expression mirrored innocence. "Why would you say that?"

"Because it's true? When you want something, you don't play coy—you go after it. I saw that when you came into the bowling alley in that little nothing of a dress. Every normal man there was checking you out. Yours truly included."

Lucy laughed softly. "I did get your attention, and it worked, didn't it?"

"That wasn't the only thing that stood up at attention." He lowered his eyes, staring at his groin.

A soft gasp escaped Lucy. "No, you didn't go there."

Calum looked up and noticed a rush of color suffusing her face. "Did I embarrass you, bae?" She averted her head and looked out the passenger's-side window. One of the many things that attracted him to Lucy was his inability to sort out exactly who she was. She had so many different sides to her personality. For Calum, that was a good thing because he knew she would never bore him. A yip from the back seat reminded him that they were there for a reason—and it wasn't so he could flirt with her.

"Come on, sweetheart. Let's get your babies inside so everyone can admire their outfits."

Lucy waited for Calum to unload Buttercup and the puppies from the SUV's cargo area, and attached leashes to their harnesses. It'd been a struggle to get the puppies to hold still long enough for her to put on their knitted doggie sweaters, designed to make them look like calves. By contrast, Buttercup had stood perfectly still when she'd put the white hoodie with black spots on her to play the role of mother cow. She'd added the horns even though the pattern didn't call for them.

"Look at the cows, Mommy," shouted a young boy who appeared to be around four or five.

The boy's mother cradled a dachshund puppy to her chest. "They're not cows, Danny. They are dogs dressed up like cows."

"They look like cows to me."

Lucy shared a smile with the mother. Once she'd made the decision to donate knitted sweaters for the various puppies and kittens, she'd decided she didn't want nonspecific sweaters but costumes. She'd knitted one in plaid to represent the Highlands, one in red and green for Santa's puppy helper for the Christmas season, a black and yellow bumblebee, and even a tweedy pattern for a Sherlock Holmes replica. And knowing she'd wanted Buttercup and the puppies to have matching ensembles, Lucy'd eventually found a pattern for a cow and her calves.

"It looks as if our furry family is already getting attention," Calum said in her ear.

"I don't know how many dachshunds will be here today, but I did knit a sweater that looks like a hot-dog bun."

"Where do you come up with these ideas?"

Lucy looped the leashes for Fritter and Waffle around her right wrist, and Pancake and Grits around the left, while Calum held on to Buttercup and Beignet. "When you teach kindergarten and first grade, you learn to be creative to spark their imaginations."

"Does that mean *our* baby will be super imaginative?"

She noticed there was a measure of pride in Calum's voice as he'd said *our baby*, as if they had picked all six winning lotto numbers.

"I don't know, Calum. Children develop their own personalities in ways that are impossible to predict." Fritter began tugging on the leash. "I think it's time we go in, because the puppies are getting antsy."

The fundraiser was in full swing with Bethany Robeson—the shelter's director—welcoming everyone. Lucy felt twin emotions of excitement and sadness. On the one hand, she knew with so many people in attendance, the fundraiser was certain to be a success, which was great. But on the other hand, the more people who saw Buttercup and her puppies, the more people would want to adopt them. The time was growing closer when the dogs would go to their forever homes.

Shane Dupree was selling T-shirts and other donations under his Barkyard Boarding tent. He beckoned Lucy over, pointing to the knitted dog sweaters. "Regina told me you donated most of these. Have you thought of starting up a business and selling them?"

Lucy smiled and shook her head. "No. I hardly have enough time with running the bookstore and with…" Her words trailed off.

Attractive laugh lines fanned out around Shane's blue eyes when he smiled. "And with a new one on the way," he said, completing her statement. He glanced at something over her shoulder. "Here comes the papa-to-be with Buttercup and one of her pups."

Lucy turned to find Calum approaching the tent.

She pointed to the sweaters lined up on the table. "These are some of my donations."

Shane shook hands with Calum. "They've been selling like crazy. I told your girlfriend that she should set up a company and sell them."

Calum gave her a sidelong glance. "I don't want to speak for Lucy. That must be her decision. Meanwhile I'd like to buy a couple of T-shirts."

"How many do you want?" Shane asked.

"How many do you have?"

"Dozens. Why?"

Lucy met Calum's eyes, wondering what he was thinking. He'd said something about making a donation. Was this how he'd chosen to help the shelter out? "I'll take three dozen in different sizes. Maybe one of these days I'll host a fundraiser day for Furever Paws at Pins and Pints. All the bowling alley employees will wear the shirts and I'll donate ten percent of the day's proceeds back to the shelter." He removed a credit card case from the front pocket of his jeans and handed one to Shane.

Shane's smile was dazzling as he tapped keys on a calculator before swiping Calum's card on a reader and returning it to him. "I'm certain that will go over big with Bunny and Birdie. I'll pack up the shirts and make certain someone will deliver them to the bowling alley in a couple of days."

"That was very generous of you," Lucy whispered to Calum as they left the tent.

"You shamed me into supporting the fundraiser."

"I didn't shame you, Calum."

He smiled. "Then let's say you inspired me."

They continued to walk around, taking in everything there was to see. "Oh, look, Calum," she said, pointing to an adorable black-and-white cockapoo. She was so caught up in admiring the other dog that she didn't notice right away that people were gathering around Buttercup and her litter of pups.

Realization finally arrived when a woman with two teenaged girls tapped her arm. "Are these puppies up for adoption?"

Lucy felt as if someone had reached inside her chest and squeezed her heart, making it impossible for her to draw a normal breath. "Yes, they are," she said in a breathless voice.

"What are their names?" asked one of the girls."

Lucy shared a glance with Calum. "The mother is Buttercup, and her puppies are Pancake, Fritter, Waffle, Grits and Beignet."

The other daughter grabbed her mother's arm. "Can we put in applications for two of them, Mom?"

"Please, please, please," her sister pleaded.

Their mother nodded. "Okay."

Lucy managed to keep her emotions in check

when she came face to face with Declan Hoyt—a local horse breeder—and his fiancée Josie Whitaker, who was a dedicated shelter volunteer and who had catered the whole party for the fundraiser. Shannon, Declan's niece, was showing off Harlow, her beautiful cockapoo puppy.

"It looks as if Harlow likes one of your puppies," Shannon teased.

"That's Fritter," Lucy said.

Declan curved an arm around his niece's waist. "If we didn't have Harlow, I'd definitely adopt one of Buttercup's puppies."

"A lot of people are looking at them," Shannon remarked.

Lucy wanted to tell the green-eyed teenaged girl with long, dark red hair she was more than aware of the intense interest in the five puppies, which made the reality of losing them feel like it was knocking at the door. This was Lucy's first time fostering a pregnant dog and her emotions were all over the place—not helped by the hormonal changes going on within her own body.

Lucy led the puppies over to where kittens were on exhibit for adoption. She recognized Brooklyn Hobbs playing with several kittens and overheard her mother telling her she could adopt one. The little girl shook her head and said she didn't want another cat—that someday Oliver would come home to her. Brooklyn reminded Lucy of one of her former students with her dark brown hair cut in a perfect bob and a fringe of adorable bangs.

She hoped the little girl's cat would find its way home. On several occasions, people would come into Chapter One claiming they'd spotted the orange cat around the outskirts of Spring Forest, but no one had been able to catch it.

She leaned close to the child's mother. "I hope she gets Oliver back soon," she whispered to Renee Hobbs.

Renee nodded. "Me, too. Oh, I meant to tell you that Brooklyn loves coming to the bookstore. She's been going through books so fast lately. Reading keeps her mind off Oliver," Renee said sotto voce.

"Good for her."

Lucy smiled when she saw Birdie Whitaker heading in her direction. Although she was smiling, Lucy detected a sadness in the green eyes of the co-owner of Whitaker Acres and co-president of Furever Paws Animal Rescue, and wondered if it was because of her breakup with the local retired vet, Doc J.

"It appears as if the fundraiser is a big success," Lucy remarked. She glanced down at the four puppies that had settled down to sleep despite the noise and excitement going on around them.

"So far, so good," Birdie agreed. "Regina may have organized it, but it looks as if her niece Elise is running herself ragged doing all the work." She waved a hand as if dismissing the outspoken thought. "What about you, Lucy?"

"What about me, Birdie?"

"How are you feeling?"

"I'm fine."

"When's the big day?"

Lucy was suddenly confused. "Big day for what?"

"Why are we playing Twenty Questions, Lucy Tucker?" Birdie snapped. "When are you expecting your baby?"

Oh, that's what she meant, Lucy thought. "Mid-February."

"That's right after the holiday season. I hope you don't plan to overdo it so close to when you have to deliver."

"I'm fortunate to have two incredibly helpful assistants."

"You are fortunate, and so are we. If it wasn't for the ongoing generosity of volunteers and donations, I doubt whether we would be able to take in so many rescues. Bunny has been over the moon at the response to this fundraiser. In case you didn't know it, my sister has a weakness for helping any animal in need, so she's thrilled about the funds to be able to do more."

Lucy wanted to point out to Birdie that her sister wasn't the only one in the family with a weakness for animals in need. Birdie might be less effusive about it, but there was no denying the two sisters' hearts were in the same place. It was why they'd donated so much of their time and resources to sheltering every animal in need they came across.

"Are you certain she's the only sister with a weakness for animals in need?" Lucy said teasingly. "I've heard that you have pigs, goats, a couple of llamas and a milk cow on Whitaker Acres."

An attractive blush spread over the tall, thin woman. Birdie lowered her bright green eyes. "I suppose I can't put all the blame on Bunny." She blew out a soft sigh. "I love animals, too."

Lucy suspected she also loved Doc J, otherwise they wouldn't have moved in together. Although he'd left for Florida, ending the relationship as far as anyone in town could tell, she hoped one day they would be able to work through their differences and reconcile. In spite of everything, Lucy was still a romantic at heart.

"Oh, before I forget, Lucy. Those pet beds you crocheted were snapped up within minutes. I know you're busy, but is it possible for you to make a few for us to sell in the gift shop? I don't mind paying for the supplies you'll need."

"I'll have to let you know." Lucy wanted to say yes, yet knew she couldn't commit to anything just now.

"No pressure, Lucy."

"Have you approached any other people who knit or crochet?"

Birdie smiled. "Just what are you hatching in that beautiful head of yours?"

"Have you heard that a book club meets at Chapter One once a month?"

"Why, yes. One of our volunteers is a member." Birdie paused, appearing deep in thought. "I see where you're going with this, Lucy. Bunny and I can put together a knitting club here at Furever Paws. I'll have to talk to my nephew Grant to see if there's money in the budget to purchase the supplies the knitters will need." She clasped her hands together. "Brains and beauty. Calum is a lucky man to have found you."

It was Lucy's turn to blush. She believed she and Calum were equally lucky to have found each other. While she still had some uncertainties about how a relationship would work out between the two of them, there was no doubt in her mind that he was special. If nothing else, she'd seen proof of it when he'd come to her house to assist with Buttercup whelping her puppies. She'd watched in awe as he'd cleaned a few of the puppies, suctioned their little mouths and helped them find a teat to nurse. For a man his size, he'd been incredibly gentle with the tiny pups.

"I think I'll keep him."

Birdie gave her an incredulous stare. "You better or some of these women that have been throwing themselves at him ever since he opened Pins and Pints will snatch him up, baby or no baby."

Lucy knew perfectly well how much attention he drew. She'd seen it whenever they were out together. When they were just friends, she'd told herself that it didn't bother her—even though it always had. And now they were something more…although they'd never actually settled on what that was. Her grammie would've told her to put on her big girl panties and face the situation head-on and do what was necessary to resolve her dilemma, but she couldn't quite bring herself to yet. Something was still holding her back.

"Speaking of your gorgeous boyfriend. He's heading this way."

Lucy turned and smiled at Calum. Buttercup's tail was wagging as she detected her sleeping puppies. Pancake stood up and barked at Beignet, and soon there was a chorus of barking coming from the litter.

"I can't believe they were so quiet a few minutes ago," Birdie remarked.

"That's because Beignet and Pancake weren't together," Lucy explained, smiling. "The two girls are the last to fall asleep and the first to wake everyone in the morning. Meanwhile their brothers are as chill as their mother."

Birdie nodded. "That's good to know for when we place them in their forever homes. If the girls are that energetic then they'll have to go homes with children."

Lucy knew Buttercup and the puppies would eventually be adopted, but to hear it come from the owner of the animal rescue facility made it even more real. She felt tears prick the backs of her eyelids and she blinked them back before they fell.

Calum watched Lucy's smile fade, replaced by an expression of sadness. Then he noticed the moisture filling her eyes and he knew it was time for them to leave. "Birdie, we have to leave now."

"Thank you for coming and for supporting Furever Paws."

"We were glad to help any way we can." He switched Beignet's leash to his left hand and rested his right at the small of Lucy's back. "Let's go home, bae."

They made it to the parking lot where he loaded the dogs into the cargo area. Lucy was already seated when he slipped in behind the wheel. "Are you all right?"

She put a hand over her mouth.

Calum told himself he had to remain calm even as his mind raced through a million scenarios of pregnancy complications that could be causing her current state. "Do you have to throw up?"

"No," Lucy said through her fingers. "I just want to go home."

He didn't know whether she wanted to go to her house or his, but since she hadn't specified—and

since she'd agreed to spend the weekend with him—
he decided on the latter.

When they arrived, Lucy had unbuckled her belt
and was out of the SUV within seconds of Calum
shutting off the engine.

"I need to lie down," she said as he unlocked the
front door.

Calum prayed she wasn't in pain and that nothing
was wrong with the baby. He returned to the SUV
and got Buttercup and her puppies inside. Once they
were settled in the mudroom, he took the stairs two
at a time and walked into the guest bedroom.

Lucy lay on the bed, her back to him. Calum stood
there, experiencing a frustrating, heartbreaking rush
of utter helplessness. Slowly, quietly, he walked to
the bed and sat, resting a hand on her shoulder.

"What's the matter, sweetheart?"

"I don't want to lose them."

His brow furrowed. Calum leaned over her. "Lose
who? Talk to me, bae."

"The puppies. So many people want to adopt them
and, when they're gone, I'll be alone again."

Taking off his boots, Calum got into bed, next
to her. They lay together like spoons. "You're never
going to be alone. You have me and that little baby
growing inside you. We're a family, Lucy. You, me
and our little one."

"Really?"

He went completely still. "You don't believe me, Lucy?"

For a long beat, there was just the sound of their measured breathing before she whispered, "It wouldn't be the first time I'd be left alone."

Calum reached over, flicked on the bedside lamp and then shifted Lucy until they were facing each other. He felt his stomach do flip-flops at the sight of her tears.

"Why do you believe I'd leave you?"

She closed her eyes and breathed out a ragged sigh.

He could tell she wanted him to drop it, but it felt like they needed to have it out, so he kept pressing. "I've spent more than a year trying to get close to you. Do you actually believe I'd leave you now that we're going to become parents?"

"That was a mistake, Calum."

It took a moment before he could manage to speak calmly. "Did your mother ever call you a mistake?"

Lucy's eyes went wide. "No. But—"

"But nothing," he countered, cutting her off. "Your mother may have had a relationship with a man who was committed to someone else, but she had you because, to her, you weren't a mistake. Your parents weren't having sex, Lucy. They had made love and, out of that love, you were created. We may have had unprotected sex, but at no time did I consider it just sex. We made love to each other."

He cradled her face. "When we first met, you don't know how I struggled not to cross the line. Everything about you communicated you wanted a friend and not a romantic relationship. It was so hard to hold myself back, but I tried to convince myself I wasn't ready for marriage and a family anyway. Once you told me you were pregnant, I realized I'd been in denial. You told me it shouldn't be up to some woman to change my mind about commitment, and you were right. After I met you, my mind changed all on its own. It was as if I'd waited all my life for someone like you to become a part of my life."

Lucy shivered as if she'd fallen through thin ice. She couldn't believe Calum had just uttered the same kinds of emotional declarations about love and life-long partnership that Johnny had made to her the night he'd proposed marriage. Was it possible, she thought, that all men read the same playbook—learned the same lines to spout what they believed women wanted to hear?

"I don't believe you, Calum," she said in a quiet voice.

He went still. "Why not?"

"Because my fiancé said the very same things to me when he asked me to marry him. And then he ran off and married my best friend instead."

Calum sat up, pulling her up to sit between his outstretched legs. "Tell me about it."

Chapter Fourteen

Lucy's voice was void of emotion when she told Calum how she'd met Johnny, fallen in love with him and agreed to marry him. She admitted that she'd envisioned a whole future with him, even though they had planned to wait a couple of years after they were married to start a family.

"I believed every word that came out of his lying mouth because I so wanted my life to be different from my mother's. I wanted my marriage to be the result of a deliberate choice."

Calum rested a hand over her middle. "Did he explain to you why he married your friend?"

She slowly shook her head. "I never spoke to him once I discovered he'd eloped with Danielle. What's so ironic is both my mother and grandmother had warned me about Danielle. They saw something in her I'd refused to see after all those years of friendship. Grammie said she was too clingy, that we'd spend too much time together. Then she reminded me of an old saying about even tongue and teeth fall out.

"As we got closer to the wedding day, my mother warned me that Johnny and Danielle were hanging out a bit too often. I questioned Danielle about it, but she said they were just discussing plans for the wedding. I thought she meant *my* wedding."

"When in reality they were talking about their own wedding plans," Calum said.

"Yup."

Calum shook his head. "That's some lowdown underhanded crap."

"I agree."

"What did your father do?"

"He told me it was better Johnny cheated on me before we married rather than after." Lucy knew her father was disappointed he hadn't been able to walk her down the aisle and give her away in marriage, but that hadn't made his uncaring words any easier to swallow.

"If some man did to my daughter what this loser did to you, I'd become the Liam Neeson character in *Taken*, when he said, 'I will look for you, I will find you and I will kill you.'"

Lucy glanced over her shoulder. "You're kidding,

aren't you?" A beat passed and then a half-smile lifted one corner of his mouth and she was finally able to relax.

"I'm only kidding about killing him. But I *would* hunt him down."

"I don't like violence, Calum."

He pressed a kiss to her nape. "Neither do I. I just need you to know that I will always protect you and our children."

Lucy couldn't stop laughing. "First it's a child and now you talk about children. Please let me push out this baby before you talk about me having more than one."

"Didn't you say that you and your ex talked about having children after a few years of marriage?"

"Yes, but by that point, we were engaged and planning a future together," Lucy admitted. At the time, she'd believed she and Johnny would spend the rest of their lives together. "That was then, and this is now. Not only did things change, but *I've* also changed, Calum. I find it much harder to trust people now—men *and* women. Haven't you noticed that since moving here, I haven't made friends with any women my age? Even with you, I did everything I possibly could to keep you at a distance."

Calum pressed his mouth to the side of her neck. "I figured you didn't have time to make friends with running the bookstore and then fostering Buttercup. And as for us being friends, I actually enjoyed it because it was the first time I'd truly been friends with a woman with nothing else mixed in."

"Are you telling me that you've slept with every woman you're friendly with?"

"No, Lucy. I've dated women I didn't sleep with for several reasons. But I never ended up being friends with them."

Lucy rested the back of her head against Calum's shoulder. "When I'd accepted Johnny's proposal, I'd believed I was ready to become a wife and mother. Then…"

"Then what?" Calum asked when her words trailed off.

"Then when the fairy-tale world I'd created for myself crumbled, I was forced to acknowledge even if I'd had one child, I would've been stuck with two."

"Your ex had a child?"

"No," she said, laughing. "*He* was the child himself. Underneath his brilliant legal mind and tailored suits was an adult-child needing constant reassurance and validation. Whenever we had an argument, it was about his lack of confidence. I believe the straw that broke the proverbial camel's back was when I told him to read *The Little Engine That Could* and a week later, exactly one month before our wedding day, he eloped with my maid of honor."

Calum buried his face in Lucy's hair. "So, instead of seeking counseling for his insecurities, he ran off with your best friend."

"Yes. Whenever I'd suggested he needed to see a therapist, he'd say there was nothing wrong with him, that I didn't understand him, or that everything would be fine if I was a more supportive partner."

"Were you devastated when he left you?"

"Devastated? No. I was humiliated. Danielle and I taught at the same school. I found out later that many of my colleagues knew what was going on between Danielle and Johnny. And, of course, everyone knew once the wedding was canceled. There was no hiding from it. My mother was devastated when I told her I was leaving Charlotte, but I had to get away from all of that."

"Charlotte's loss is Spring Forest's gain in more ways than one."

Lucy extricated herself from Calum's hold, turning around to sit facing him. "Lucky me," she whispered. Attractive lines appeared around his eyes when he smiled.

"Lucky us." She pressed her breasts against his chest and then gasped from the pleasurable sensations shooting through them.

Calum's arms tightened around her back. The pressure of Lucy's hips against his groin made it impossible for him to restrain his growing erection, and he wondered if she was aware of what she was doing. "What's the matter?" he asked, registering her heavy, shuddering breaths as she buried her face between his neck and shoulder.

"My breasts," she whispered.

"What about them?"

"They're very sensitive."

He reached under her shirt and gently cradled one, smiling when he heard her intake of breath. "Does this hurt?"

The seconds ticked before Lucy said, "It's sort of a good hurt."

"How about this?" Calum's thumb swept over a distended nipple under silk and lace, eliciting another gasp from Lucy. He squeezed her breast a little tighter and this time she moaned. A moan he remembered when they'd made love what now seemed eons ago.

"Please," she whispered in his ear.

Calum smothered his own groan. "Please what, bae?"

Her breathing was coming faster as he massaged her breasts. "Please don't make me beg you."

"For what?"

"To make love to me."

Calum did not understand why Lucy thought of herself as alone. She had Buttercup and her puppies. She had her baby. She had him. "You will never be alone." *Not if there is breath in my body*, he swore to himself. She might not be willing to believe his declaration, but that didn't make it any less true.

She'd demonstrated her vulnerability when she'd revealed why she'd fled Charlotte for Spring Forest, and it was that vulnerability Calum didn't want to take advantage of if they were to make love. "Are you certain, Lucy?" he asked, wanting and needing her consent.

"Yes, I am certain."

He reversed their positions, hovering above her, and slowly removed her clothes. Their gazes met, fused as he watched her reaction to his undressing her. He sucked in a lungful of breath when seeing her completely nude. Her breasts were fuller than they had been the last time he'd done this, her waist wider, and he curbed the urge to sample every inch of her ripening lush body. Calum undressed quickly, smiling when Lucy opened her arms.

Lucy's breath slowed to a measured rhythm, belaying the rush of desire racing headlong throughout her body. She curved her arms under his broad shoulders as Calum lowered his body, aligning it with her form until his mouth was inches from hers. What had begun as a gentle brushing of lips deepened until she felt his weight pressing her down to the mattress. There was a sweet, deep intimacy to their kisses.

A haze of passion swept over Lucy, her mind reeling with questions she was unable to answer. Did she love this man? But more importantly, could she trust the father of her unborn child? She closed her eyes as the warmth flooding her body increased, sweeping down and settling between her thighs while bringing a fiery hotness that made it impossible for her to remain motionless.

The heat from Calum's mouth swept to her own and then to her core. Waves of passion wracked her until she could not stop her legs from shaking. He suckled her breasts, worshipping them, and the moans she sought to muffle escaped her parted lips. His tongue circled her nipples, leaving them hard, erect and throbbing before his teeth nipped the turgid tips, and she felt a violent spasm grip her womb.

Lucy registered a series of breathless sighs, not realizing at first that they were her own moans of physical satisfaction. Eyes closed, head thrown back, lips parted, back arched, she reveled in the sensations taking her beyond herself when she felt Calum inside her.

Calum slowly eased his erection into Lucy, sighing when he fully sheathed himself inside her. He smiled when her arms went from his shoulders to around his neck as their bodies found and set a rhythm where they were in perfect harmony. Reaching down, he cupped her hips, lifting her higher and permitting deeper penetration; then he quickened his movements.

Lucy assisted him by circling her legs around his waist. His love and passion for her rose higher and higher until it exploded in an awesome, vibrating liquid fire that left them both convulsing in scorched ecstasy.

There was only the sound of their labored breathing in the stillness of the bedroom as they lay motionless, savoring the aftermath of a shared, sweet fulfillment. Calum could not believe the passion Lucy aroused in him; if possible, he wanted to make love to her all through the night.

Reluctantly, he pulled out and lay beside her. He reached for her hand, threading their fingers together.

Calum had known Lucy was special the moment she'd introduced herself. What he hadn't known was how special she would become to him, or that he'd fall in love with her pretty much at first sight.

However, love wasn't as important to Lucy as trust, and he knew he had to work hard to get her to truly, fully trust him. More importantly, he had to convince her that he would never leave or cheat on her.

"Are you okay?" he asked when she turned to face him.

"I'm better than okay."

Calum released her hand and draped an arm over her waist. "Don't bother to get up early tomorrow morning. I'll bring you breakfast in bed."

Lucy rubbed her nose against his chin. "You're going to spoil me."

He laughed softly. "That's my intent."

"I think I'm going to keep you, Calum Ramsey."

"And that goes double for me, Lucy Tucker."

Calum cradled her to his chest as her breathing slowed until she fell asleep.

He wanted her and the baby. Someday, somehow, he'd prove to her that his feelings were lasting and real. Until then, he'd just have to keep showing her, in every way that he could.

Lucy stirred slightly but didn't wake up when he lifted her off the bed and carried her into his bedroom.

Then he returned to the en suite bath in the guest room and brought all her personal and grooming items into his bathroom. He'd decided to wait to broach the subject of turning the guest bedroom into a nursery.

Calum took a quick shower and then slipped into bed beside Lucy.

"Come in," Calum said when he heard someone knocking on the door. "What is it, Timmy?" he asked.

"Ms. Fowler and Miss Grace need you to come to the bookstore."

Calum jumped to his feet, his heart pounding in his chest. He didn't want to think about what could have happened to Lucy. The one time he'd mentioned she was doing too much, she'd warned him to stay out of her business. But she *was* his business because she was carrying his child.

"Tell whoever is at the bar to take the calls."

It took less than three minutes for Calum to leave the bowling alley and walk into Chapter One. "Where is she?" he asked Miss Grace when he didn't see Lucy at the front.

"She's in the back with Angela. I told her she was doing too much, but she just won't listen."

Calum heard the uneasiness in the woman's voice and wanted to tell her she wasn't alone in believing Lucy was overdoing it. He nodded to a man sitting in the reading corner and headed to the store's office door. He knocked and Angela Fowler opened it after he'd identified himself.

"Where is she?"

"She's in the storeroom," the retired librarian whispered. "I told her I would unpack the boxes, but she wasn't having any of it. Then after, she took the dogs for a walk even though she'd complained of feeling lightheaded. She looked ready to pass out by the time she got back, and that's when we made her lie down."

Calum barely glanced at Buttercup and her puppies sleeping behind an enclosure. "Thank you for looking after her, Ms. Fowler."

"You don't have to thank me, Calum. Lucy is like a daughter to me."

Calum smiled. Then he opened the door to the

storeroom and found Lucy, eyes closed on a deck chair. Hunkering down next to her, he touched her hand. Her eyes opened and she gave him a weak smile.

"How are you feeling?" he asked.

"Better."

"Did you eat?"

Lucy's eyelids fluttered. "Not yet."

Calum reminded himself not to snap at her even as he clamped his jaw shut in frustration. She'd been instructed to eat at least five small meals a day. "Do you feel like eating now?"

"Yes. Who told you I was back here?"

"Ms. Fowler and Miss Grace told Timmy to get me."

A frown settled into Lucy's features as she sat up straight. "So now you have my assistants snitching on me?"

"It's not snitching, Lucy."

"You know what they say about snitches, don't you?"

"Yeah," he drawled, "they get stitches. No one is getting cut here." Calum stood. "I'm going to get the lunch Timmy brought over for you. Then I'll take you home so you can rest for a while. I also plan to take over fostering Buttercup. You can come over and see her whenever you want, but I don't want you wearing yourself out looking after her."

"What about the puppies?"

"Now that they're close to being weaned, two of them can go to another foster. Which three do you want to keep?" Calum knew if he didn't allow Lucy to make that her choice, she would bring holy hell down on him.

"Fritter, Pancake and Beignet."

He smiled. "I'll call the shelter and have them send someone to pick up Waffle and Grits." Curving an arm around her back, Calum helped Lucy to her feet. "After you eat something, you'll feel better."

"It just came down on me so suddenly, Calum."

He dropped a kiss on her hair. "I know, bae. That's why eating is more important than unpacking boxes or walking dogs."

She flashed a weak smile. "I know that now."

It didn't take long to get used to his new routine now that he was fostering Buttercup. The golden retriever really was easy to care for—and it was surprisingly soothing to come home to her.

Lucy had brought the three remaining puppies over to see their mother, who had begun pushing them away when they attempted to suckle. With them almost fully weaned, he knew they would soon be put up for adoption.

"Calum, you're not paying attention to a word I've been saying."

"I'm sorry, bae, but my mind was elsewhere." He glanced at the laptop she had in front of her with images of baby cribs. "Isn't it a little early to think about buying baby furniture?"

"I'm not buying anything now. I'm just planning for how I want to decorate the nursery. Of course, I'll have to give up having a guest bedroom."

He gave her a long, penetrating stare. "You're thinking of turning the guest room in the rental into a nursery?"

Lucy continued scrolling through options. "Yes. Why?"

"Because I thought we'd set up the nursery here."

Her fingers stilled on the keyboard as she slowly turned her head to meet his eyes. "When were you going to mention this to me?"

"I just did."

Lucy blew out her breath. "That's something we should've discussed before you assumed the nursery would be at your place."

Calum crossed his arms over his chest, readying himself to state his case.

"Think about it, bae. If you decide to spend more time at my house, where do you expect the baby to sleep? Every child should have its own room, and there's more than enough space here for that."

"You're right," Lucy said after a moment of strained silence. "How do you plan to decorate the nursery?"

"That will be your decision. You can decorate

the room by yourself, or I can contact a decorator to work with you."

There came another pause before she said, "Maybe she can take a look at both my rental and here. That way, we can have a consistent theme across the two nurseries."

Calum lowered his arms, moved closer to Lucy and draped one over her shoulders when she logged off and closed the laptop. He wondered if she would ever accept his offer for them to live together. When he'd asked whether she would live with a man, she'd admitted it would depend on the man. Well, he wasn't just any man, but her lover and the father of her unborn child.

Patience, Ramsey. He'd told himself over and over to be patient with Lucy. If they were going to live together, then that would have to be her decision. It would be the same with an engagement and wedding.

"Are you planning to spend the night or are you going home?" he asked.

Lucy laid her head against his shoulder. "I think I'm going to stay. I ate too much, and I'd probably fall asleep behind the wheel before making it home. Besides, the puppies need to spend as much time with Buttercup as they can before they go to their forever homes."

Calum smiled as he combed his fingers through her hair. "I was hoping you would say that." He was getting used to Lucy spending nights at his house.

"Aiden doesn't mind working the night shift?"

"Aiden prefers working nights."

Calum arrived at Pins and Pints at nine—two hours before it opened for business—and left around six, while Aiden came in at five thirty and worked until closing. They were so in sync that that half hour of overlap was all they needed to check in and pass off any important information, such as ideas for new events for the bowling alley. When he'd pitched hosting a fundraiser for Furever Paws Animal Rescue to Aiden, his assistant manager had suggested recruiting local businesses to form teams to compete for first-, second- and third-place trophies. It was a great idea—one he was looking forward to putting into effect.

"What do you want for breakfast?" Calum asked Lucy.

"Shrimp and grits."

"Hey now," Calum said, smiling. "You're singing my song. I just happen to have a bag of extra-large frozen shrimp in the freezer."

She angled her head. "I don't know why, but I've been craving shrimp and grits and gelato."

Calum nibbled the side of her neck. "I don't have any gelato on hand, but I'll try and get some for you. Any particular flavor?"

"Vanilla, hazelnut, pistachio, peach or orange."

"You prefer gelato to ice cream?"

Lucy moaned as he continued to kiss her neck.

"Yes. It's lighter than ice cream because it's made with custard and less butterfat, and that makes the flavors more intense. During my stay in Italy, I ate it practically every day."

"Do you have any other cravings?"

"That's it for now. And I promise not to ask you to get up at one in the morning to go and get me some pickles and potato chips." Lucy reached under her shirt and loosened the drawstring on her shorts.

Calum took the computer off her lap and placed it on the floor before anchoring a hand under her knees and shifting her until her legs rested across his thighs. "Are you more comfortable now?"

Lucy rested her back against the padded arm of the love seat. "Yes. I need to go online and order some stretchy pants."

"How much weight have you gained?"

"Four pounds, so far. And it all seems to be in my middle. Give me a few more months and I'll look as if I swallowed a melon."

Calum massaged her legs. "You'll look even more beautiful than you do now. There's nothing more beautiful than ripened fruit. Look how many famous artists used fruit in their still life paintings."

"I believe it all came down to money, Calum," Lucy countered. "They were known as starving artists for a reason. If they wanted a live person to pose for them, they would have to feed and/or pay them.

Fruit was less demanding. And once they finished with the painting, they could eat it."

"You would come up with that rationale."

Lucy scrunched up her nose. "You'd have to agree that it's plausible." She closed her eyes for several seconds. "There was a time when I wondered what it would've been like for me live in a Parisian garret with my struggling painter lover where we'd exist on cheese, wine and freshly baked baguettes."

"And what would you be doing with your painter lover?"

"Posing for his paintings, many of them in the nude, and then we would make endless love."

Calum's mouth twitched in amusement before becoming a wide grin. "You really have a very vivid imagination."

Her eyebrows lifted. "You've never imagined living in another era?"

"No, bae. I like where I am, what I'm doing and who I'm with. I wouldn't change my life for anything because it would mean not being with you." Calum knew he'd shocked Lucy with his impassioned statement. And he knew it was just a matter of time before he would have to reveal to her the depths of his feelings not only for her but for the child growing beneath her heart.

Lucy sat straight. "I think I'm going to turn in now. Saturdays are always busy at the store."

Calum helped her off the love seat. He hoped he

hadn't come on too strong. He'd decided to let things unfold naturally. Lucy wasn't leaving Spring Forest, and neither was he.

"I'm going to take Buttercup and the puppies for their last walk then I'll be up after that."

Lucy was usually in bed asleep when he finally turned in for the night. The warmth from her body, the lingering scent of her bodywash from her shower and the crush of her fuller breasts against his chest would send his libido into overdrive only to have it assuage with early morning lovemaking. It was a routine he would happily continue forever.

There was no place, no time he'd rather be than here. And if he were to imagine anything, it would be for them to grow old together.

Chapter Fifteen

Calum was used to families coming to Pins and Pints on Saturday mornings, but lately he'd taken more of an interest in seeing parents interact with their children now that he was going to be a father.

He approached Ian Parsons when he walked in with his young twin daughters.

"Welcome to Pins and Pints," he said, greeting Ian with a smile and handshake.

Ian released one daughter's hand and shook Calum's. "Thanks. I heard that you'll soon become a papa."

"You heard right."

Calum hunkered down until he was almost eye-level with the little girls with white-blond hair and huge blue eyes. "Hello. I'm Calum."

One of the girls smiled. I'm Abby."

"It's nice meeting you, Abby." He turned his attention to her sister, who'd looked away rather than meet his eyes. "And who are you?"

"She's Annie," Abby said. "She doesn't talk."

Ian frowned at his daughter. "Abby." The single word, though spoken softly, held a hint of a warning. "It's nice seeing you again, Calum."

"Same here."

He watched Ian lead his children to the shoe rental and then stop when a woman said something to Abby. A shock raced through Calum when he heard the little girl tell the woman her mother was dead. He didn't know why, but he'd assumed Ian was divorced, since it was clear that the man was raising his children on his own.

The reality that Ian had lost his children's mother was a wake-up call for Calum. It reminded him that he had no way of guaranteeing Lucy and their child's future. He wanted to believe that everything would work out fine, but what if it didn't? He returned to his office and placed a call to his insurance company and then another to the law office that handled his personal legal affairs. If something were to happen to him, he would feel better knowing they would be financially protected.

Lucy sent him a text saying she was going to stay

home to do laundry and clean the house, and she would see him in a couple of days. Calum stared at his phone, rereading the message and feeling a little unsettled. It wasn't like Lucy not to give him a definitive date when they would see each other again.

Before he knew it, it was late afternoon and the atmosphere inside Pins and Pints changed as the clientele started shifting from families with young children to teenagers and adults. Calum had had a long conversation with his insurance agent outlining the changes in his life insurance policy. The receptionist at the law office said she would relay his message to his attorney, who would get back to him after the weekend.

Aiden had come in and Calum was preparing to leave when Harris Vega walked up and greeted him with a wide grin. "Come sit with me for a while."

Calum stared at the house flipper. His light brown eyes were dancing with merriment. "That grin tells me you're pleased about something." Harris pulled him over to the bar and signaled for the bartender to bring him a drink. "What are you celebrating?"

Harris ran a hand over his stubble. "I just sold the house Bethany Robeson inherited and I managed to flip it for a pretty penny."

Calum patted his back. "Good for you. And again, I want to thank you for helping with the terms for Lucy's lease renewal."

"Come on, man. You're talking to me. That's what

friends do." Harris paused. "I know it's none of my business, but why is she looking to renew her lease when she can move in with you now that she's having your kid?"

"How well do you know women, Harris?"

"Probably not as well as I should. That's probably why I'm still a bachelor."

Calum exchanged a fist bump with the builder. "Same here, brother. Please don't get me wrong. I'd be thrilled if Lucy moved in with me. But every time I've dropped hints, she's reacted as if I was speaking a foreign language. And the one time I proposed marriage, it was like she was at a comedy club laughing at a joke from a stand-up comedian."

"You mean she laughed at you?" Calum nodded. "Man, that's cold."

"It wasn't as cold as it was lame." He knew he had to defend Lucy. "I'd just blurted it out."

"You didn't say 'I love you' or 'Baby, you're the love of my life'? Though, come to think of it, those can come across as lame, too, if the delivery isn't right. It would sound a lot more romantic if you'd said it in Spanish."

"Maybe that works for you, but I don't speak Spanish."

Harris nodded at the bartender when he set his drink on a coaster. "Do you want to marry her?"

Calum nodded again.

"Is it about Lucy or the baby, Calum?"

"It's both," he countered quickly.

Harris lifted his drink. "I wish you luck."

"I'm going to need it." Getting Lucy to accept his proposal of marriage would be as challenging to him as attempting to climb to the top of Mount Everest.

"I haven't drawn up her renewal lease, but I'm willing to add a clause to let her rent the property on a month-to-month basis with the stipulation she gives me thirty days before she plans to move out, if she decides to move in with you."

"No, Harris. That sounds like collusion. Thanks for trying to help out, but Lucy will see right through it, especially since I told her I would speak to you about the lease. If she does sign the renewal and then moves out before it expires, I will pay the rent on the remaining months."

Harris shook his head. "That's not going to happen. I will not take your money. Consider it a gift from me to your son or daughter. Right now, I'm doing quite well financially."

"Don't even try to pay for your drink." Calum signaled the bartender. "My friend's money is no good here. But as for me, I must go home and walk my dog."

He'd grown very attached to Buttercup and had begun to think of her as his dog. She was there to greet him when he walked through the door and she followed him around from room to room. She even curled up beside him on the leather sofa when he went downstairs to watch television. Buttercup would nudge him with her nose when she wanted to be scratched behind the ears, something he'd witnessed Lucy doing on occasion. Yes, the golden retriever was spoiled, but she was too sweet for anyone to mind. He didn't want to think of the time when she would have to go to a forever home and not be in his life anymore.

Lucy sat at the table in Calum's eat-in kitchen and tried to slow the rapid beating of her heart. He'd given her an envelope with documents detailing what she would receive if he happened to pass away.

"What do I need with a two-million-dollar life insurance policy, Calum?"

"Who's to say what you might need it for? There may come a time when it will come in handy."

She combed her fingers through her hair. "Is there something you're not telling me? Are you sick?"

A smirk played at the corners of his mouth. "Not that I know of since my last physical."

"This is not funny," she snapped. "What made you draw up a will and take out an insurance policy even before our child is born?"

A frown replaced his smirk. "Because I believe in planning ahead. Don't forget my background as a financial planner and investment analyst."

Lucy threw her hands over her face as she attempted to process what Calum had shown her. She wanted to believe that he was okay, that he would be with her when she went into labor and delivered their baby. "Swear to me you're not lying about being sick," she said through her fingers.

"I'm—" His words were cut off when the chime of the doorbell echoed throughout the house.

Her hands came down. "Are you expecting company?"

"No. I'll be right back." Calum stood and walked out of the kitchen to answer the door.

Lucy continued to stare at copies of the documents spread out on the table. She and Calum hadn't talked about child support because, for her, it wasn't an issue. Both she and Calum were business owners with viable establishments, and she was sure either of them would be able to provide for their child on their own, if that ever proved necessary.

She froze when hearing raised voices. She recognized Calum's and then another man's. Soon they were yelling at each other, and Lucy stood up and went to see who it was.

Lucy felt as if she'd been jolted by a surge of electricity when she saw an older man she knew had to be Calum's father. The resemblance between the two men was remarkable.

"I don't give a damn if you have to sleep in the street. I'm not giving you any money," Calum shouted. "Where the hell were you when my mother waited every day for the bank to foreclose on the house because you didn't give a damn about making payments—even if it meant your children would be put in the street? You didn't care because you were somewhere drinking up the money you should've brought home to support your family. Now I want you to get out of my house and never come back."

"I'm not asking for much, Calum. Just a little to tide me over until I find another job."

"Do you know how tired that sounds? How many times have you sold that sob story before? You're an alcoholic and you need help."

"I'm not an alcoholic, Calum."

"Okay. Then you're a drunk. I'm not going to tell you again to leave my home."

The older man waved his arms. "Just wait until you have kids, and you fall on hard times and go to them for help. Then you'll know how it feels when they tell you to sleep in the street." Turning on his heel, he stomped out, and Calum slammed the door behind him.

Calum's hands tightened into fists and when he turned, he saw Lucy staring at him as if he were a stranger. He walked over to her. "Bae."

She took step backward. "No, Calum. Don't."

"I'm sorry you had to witness that."

"So am I. Did you have to say those awful, nasty things to him? Couldn't you have just said no and left it at that?"

"Keith Ramsey doesn't understand the word no. The man you saw is an alcoholic that refuses to acknowledge he needs help. I watched my mother make excuses for him for years until there were none left. After cashing his paycheck, he'd stop at a bar instead of coming home, and buy rounds of drinks for everyone because he thought of himself as Big Willie. Then he'd come home reeking of alcohol and claim someone had either picked his pocket or that the teller had shortchanged him at the bank."

"Your mother believed him?"

"Of course she didn't, but he was her first love and she didn't want to lose him. She literally worked her fingers to the bone at two different jobs to pay the mortgage and keep shoes on her kids' feet. She barely had time to sleep or eat. My sister and I were at risk of being taken away by child protective services because our mother simply didn't have the luxury of being home with us. The only thing that saved us from that was our grandmother selling her farm and moving in with us."

"Where was your father during this time?"

"In and out of our house like a revolving door. My father is a master mechanic. You could tell him to take apart a car's engine and then blindfold him and tell him to put it back together again and he could do it every time. He was good enough to always be able to find a job, but he never could keep one for long. I forget how many times he was fired for drinking on the job. Whenever he had money, he was MIA, but once the money was gone, he'd come home, sweet-talking my mother to take him back. It finally ended the time when he found her handbag and stole the money she had planned to deposit in the bank to pay bills. That's when I told him to either go into rehab or get out for good."

"How old were you?" Lucy asked.

"Fifteen. By that time, I was as tall as he was and had put on muscle from working out. My mother was there, pleading with me not to hit him. She didn't know I would never hit my father—luckily, he didn't know that, either. The bluff worked on him. He said he was leaving and never coming back."

Lucy put her palms together in a prayerful gesture. "Did your mother ever see him again?"

"I don't think so, otherwise she would've told me. Once she divorced him, he had to know that it was over between them."

Lucy took another step back when Calum reached for her. "There's something I don't understand, Calum."

He met her eyes. "What is it?"

"You're the son of an alcoholic, and you don't drink. Did you lie to me when I asked if you were in recovery?"

He glared at her. "No, I didn't lie. I don't drink because I don't want to end up like my father. Before he went to bed, he had to have a couple of drinks to sleep, and when he woke up, he needed a few more just to function. When you live with an alcoholic, you can either accept or reject it. I decided on the latter, Lucy. There was a time in my life when I did drink—but I saw the potential for it to get out of control, so I decided to stop altogether."

"You haven't had a drink since buying Pins and Pints?"

"I'd stopped drinking several years before buying Pins and Pints. Even when Aiden hosted parties at his penthouse and the booze flowed like water, I'd drink tonic water or club soda."

Lucy found it incredible that he'd had the will-power not to drink along with the others. "Weren't you even tempted?"

"No. Once I decided I wanted no part of that life, I switched on the no booze sign in my brain."

"Do you miss drinking?"

Calum shook his head. "No. You don't want to repeat your parents' history by marrying because you're pregnant, and I don't want to repeat history with you by becoming an alcoholic who can't take care of my family."

"Is that why you drew up that will and listed me as the beneficiary on your life insurance policy? Because you're afraid you might slip and start drinking again?"

He took a step and when he reached out to touch

her, she backed up again. "No. My fear of becoming an alcoholic has nothing to do with my need to secure your future. Tomorrow isn't promised to any of us, so I'm trying to be a responsible father even before our child is born."

"You can't rewrite history, Calum, because there's no way you can right the wrongs."

"Is it wrong that I don't want to end up like my father, Lucy? That I don't want to make your life and that of our child a living hell?"

"That will never happen."

"How can you be so certain?" Calum retorted, his voice escalating, growing louder in spite of his attempts to stay calm. "You don't understand what it was like. Even though you were raised by a single mother, your father was still in your life. You didn't have to concern yourself whether there was enough food in the fridge, or if someone would come and put boards on your house while all your worldly possessions were thrown out into the street. Your mother didn't have to hide her wallet in fear that her husband would steal her money. That's what me and my sister had to go through. Not knowing from one day to the next what damage would be done by our so-called father that loved his booze more than his wife and kids."

Lucy could feel the anger and pain underneath Calum's words. Even though it wasn't aimed at her, she didn't feel comfortable around it. "I'm going home. I...I have to admit, I had no idea you were carrying that much grief. I'm no expert, but it sounds to me like you need help dealing with unresolved issues stemming from your childhood."

"And you don't have issues, Lucy?"

She stiffened, her defenses rising up into place. "Yes, I have them, but I refuse to let them control my life."

Calum's eyes narrowed. "Oh, yeah? Then why are you using what happened between your mother and father as an excuse to stop us from becoming a family?"

She'd heard enough. "You claim to have total recall," she spat out angrily, "so it's time you rewind that tape in your head to pull up everything I've told you why I can't commit to marriage at this time in my life. It's all about trust, Calum. You want me to trust you, but you've been hiding so much from me! This is the real reason why you didn't think you were ready to be a father, isn't it? Were you ever going to tell me? Trust, Calum. Even though I love you, I still don't trust you. And I need some time away from you to figure out what I want and need."

"How much time, Lucy?"

"I don't know."

Lucy walked around him, scooped her tote off the chair in the entryway, opened the door and then closed it softly behind her. She knew she had to put some distance between her and Calum or their fragile relationship would cease to exist.

She activated the Bluetooth feature and tapped the number on the navigation screen before backing out of the town house's driveway. The ringing of a phone echoed throughout the interior of the Toyota before someone answered.

"Hi, Mom."

"What's wrong, Lucy?"

"Why do you think something's wrong?"

"I know my daughter. Whenever you're upset or stressed, your voice goes up a little."

Lucy smiled despite the turmoil going on inside her. "I suppose I can't fool you, can I?"

"No, and you should never attempt to. Talk to me, baby."

Myra calling her "baby" opened the floodgates and Lucy told her mother everything.

"I want you to listen carefully to what I'm going to say to you, Lucy, and not interrupt me until I'm finished."

"Okay, Mom."

"You may not want to admit it, but you still haven't gotten over Johnny's duplicity. If you're struggling to trust Calum you might want to take a hard look at whether that's really because he hasn't earned it or because you're refusing to give it. It does sound like he should have been more open with you, but try and put yourself in his shoes. He loves you, Lucy, and he wants to take care of you and your baby.

"I applaud him for his drawing up a will and taking out life insurance to make certain you and his child will be financially secure. It's all the more admirable because that's something his father couldn't or wouldn't do for Calum's mother and sister. Calum is not his father, and you are not your mother. The circumstances surrounding your pregnancy and mine are completely different, not least, you're a lot stronger than I was at that time in my life."

She took a breath before continuing. "I married your father because I didn't want to be one of those girls in my neighborhood having babies from different men and then struggling to raise them—alone. I knew his mother didn't like me, but I was willing to put up with her relentless denigration because I'd felt I'd made it by being his wife. I'd married into one of Charlotte's elite Black families. I'd put up with the veiled innuendos from my mother-in-law until she attacked you, Lucy. That's when all the tomfoolery came to an abrupt stop. Mess with me, but not my daughter. Once you have your baby, you will turn into a mama bear willing to die to protect her cub, and I believe it will be the same with Calum because not only will he protect you but also his child." Myra paused. "Do you love him, Lucy?"

"Yes, Mama. I love him." And she did. Lucy

wasn't certain when it had happened, yet she wasn't able to deny it.

Myra's sultry laugh filled the interior of the vehicle. "Do you realize that you've been calling me Mama more often now?"

Lucy also laughed. "Maybe a part of me wants to be a little girl again."

"You can't turn back the clock, Lucy. But you also don't have to. I don't care how old you are or how many grandbabies you give me, in some ways you'll still be my little girl."

Her eyes filled with tears and Lucy blinked them back before they fell. "What do you think I should do?"

"If you called to get things off your chest, I'm more than willing to listen. But if you want advice, then that's something I'm not ready to give you. The only thing I'm going to say is take your time, Lucy, and weigh your options. The choice is yours and you alone can decide whether you want to become a single mother. I can truthfully say it's always easier when you have a supportive partner. And a partner doesn't always mean marriage."

"Are you saying we should live together?"

"No, I'm not. That must be your and Calum's decision."

Lucy pulled into the driveway at her house. "Thank you, Mom, for letting me bend your ear."

"That's why I'm here. By the way, when am I going to see you?"

"Soon, Mom. I'm still fostering three puppies and as soon as they are adopted, I'll drive to Charlotte to spend a weekend with you and my stepfather."

"That sounds like a plan. Take care of yourself."

"I promise I will. Love you, Mom."

"Love you more."

Lucy disconnected the Bluetooth and shut off the engine. She closed her eyes and exhaled. She agreed with her mother that she should take her time before deciding about her relationship with Calum. Because right now, she had no idea what to do.

Chapter Sixteen

Lucy unloaded Fritter, Pancake and Beignet from the cargo area of her SUV for the last time. She was dropping them off at the shelter for their adoption. The night before, she'd sat on the floor while they'd crawled in and out of her lap, marveling at how much they'd grown. At ten weeks, they were completely weaned and Fritter, the largest of the litter, tipped the scale at sixteen pounds.

Calum had called, sent texts and left countless voice mails the first week following his confrontation with his father—though he'd had the sense not to confront her in person, either at home or at Chapter One. When Lucy didn't respond, they'd stopped.

Perhaps, she thought, he was finally getting the message that she needed some alone time.

She led the puppies inside, kissing each on the top of their head and then averting her eyes when the volunteer came to take them away. Lucy turned to leave before breaking down completely and nearly collided with Wendy Alvarez, who spent her free time volunteering with Pets for Vets. The tall brunette greeted her with a warm smile brightening her light green eyes.

"Look at you," Wendy crooned, smiling. "You're practically glowing. Congratulations to you and Calum on your impending bundle of joy."

Lucy returned Wendy's friendly smile. She wanted to tell Wendy she was also growing. She wasn't technically showing yet, but she could definitely tell a difference in the way her clothes fit. Even if her pregnancy wasn't evident to the eye, she was constantly aware of it.

"Thank you. Are you here to select a dog for a veteran?"

"No. I'm here to check on Jedidiah."

Lucy recalled the German shepherd puppy, named Jedidiah, who had been part of the group rescued from the backyard breeder. He'd been in particularly bad shape when they'd gotten him. "Is he okay?"

"Not yet. He's still too weak to be adopted. However, I was able to pull three of his siblings for the Pets for Vets program. They're all great dogs, but there's something about Jedidiah that tugs at my heart. That has never happened with the other dogs I've selected for the program."

Lucy knew what Wendy was talking about because it was the same with her and Buttercup. "It's comforting to know he's getting the best care available."

Wendy nodded. "That's for sure."

"I'd like to stay and chat, but I have to get back to the bookstore."

"It's okay, Lucy. One of these days we should get together and have a girl's night."

"I'd like that," Lucy said truthfully. She hadn't made friends with any woman in her age group since moving to Spring Forest, but there was something about the self-employed accountant that clicked with her. Maybe it was time to let go of the memory of Danielle's deception and let herself make friends again.

Lucy was still smiling when she returned to the parking lot and got into her vehicle. She was several minutes into her drive back to the business district when she felt cramping in her belly. "Oh, no!" she whispered as she drove quickly in the direction of her house. There was no way she wanted to throw up on the side of the road. She'd thought her morning sickness was over because she hadn't had an episode in more than a week.

She made it back to the house in record time and

raced into the bathroom to purge her stomach. The cramping continued, but nothing came up. Then she felt some moisture between her legs and when she pulled down her slacks and panties, she nearly fainted when she noticed drops of blood. She was spotting. Lucy forced herself not to panic. She found her cell phone and tapped a number. The call was answered after the first ring.

"What's up, Lucy?"

"I'm bleeding," she screamed into the mouthpiece. "Calum, I'm losing our baby!"

"Where are you?"

"I'm home," Lucy sobbed.

"I want you to listen to me, Lucy. Unlock your door and then get into bed. As soon as I hang up, I'm going to call 9-1-1. I'm on my way."

Calum reacted like an automaton after calling for an ambulance to take Lucy to the nearest hospital. He'd walked and talked at the same time, ordering Timmy to go to the bookstore to tell Lucy's assistants that she wouldn't be coming in. By the time he was in his car and heading for Lucy's house, he'd called Aiden to ask him to cover for him until further notice because he had a family emergency.

After that, hours passed and Calum lost track of time as he alternated pacing and drinking countless cups of bitter black coffee from the ER's waiting room beverage machine. He'd arrived at Lucy's house minutes before the EMTs and followed the ambulance, with flashing lights and blaring sirens, to the small private hospital several towns away. He'd also done something he hadn't in years: he'd prayed. He'd prayed not to lose Lucy, and then he'd prayed she wouldn't lose the baby.

"Mr. Ramsey."

He turned to find a young doctor standing a few feet away. His heart was pounding so hard, he wondered if the doctor could see it beating through his T-shirt.

"Yes."

"I'm Dr. Ramos. We stopped the bleeding, and Ms. Tucker is resting, but I'd like to keep her for a few days to monitor her progress."

"Did she…?"

The doctor smiled. "The baby's okay."

Calum was certain the woman heard his exhalation of relief. "When can I see her?"

"Follow me and I'll take you to her room. I want to alert you that we gave her something that made her a little drowsy, so she may be out of it for a while."

"The drug won't hurt the baby?"

Dr. Ramos smiled at him over her shoulder. "No." She stopped at the room at the end of the hallway and stepped aside. "Remember, she may not be as alert as you'd like."

Calum nodded. "Thank you, Doctor." He walked into the private room and stood at the foot of Lucy's bed. Her eyes were closed in sleep. The silence was punctuated by the discreet beeping sound of a machine monitoring her vitals.

Pulling over a chair, he sat next to the bed and touched her fingers gingerly, not wanting to disturb the IV. "I know you probably can't hear me, but I want you to know that I love you, and you're the most precious thing in my life. And my loving you has nothing to do with our baby, because I can now admit openly that I've been head-over-heels in love with you all along."

Calum paused and took a deep breath as he struggled not to lose his composure. "I'd asked myself over and over what it was about you that tied me into knots, and I still can't come up with an answer. I used to make fun of dudes that claimed they'd fallen in love with a woman at first sight, but now I know exactly what they were talking about."

He paused again. "I just knew I wanted to be near you, as often as I could, in any way you'd let me. I thought I was being subtle accepting your deliveries and then having to take them to you, but I suppose I wasn't that clever since some of my employees called me on it. They knew what I was up to all along."

He leaned forward when Lucy's eyelids fluttered, and he waited for her to wake up. Calum was still sitting in the chair watching for a sign that she was coming out of the sedative when a nurse entered the room. "I'm sorry, sir, but you're going to have to leave now. Visiting hours are over."

"What time can I come back?"

"Evening visiting hours begin again tomorrow at seven. You can come back then."

He stood. "Okay."

"Don't worry, Mr. Ramsey. We have your contact number if there is a change in her condition."

"Thank you."

Calum drove back to Spring Forest, his thoughts in tumult as he sought to figure out what he had to do to convince Lucy that he loved her, and she could trust him to take care of her and their baby. She'd asked for space and time, and he'd given her that. But now her time was up because, with her lying in a hospital bed, all the rules had changed. She needed to know that she wasn't alone, that he was with her no matter what—and that he would be for the rest of their lives.

Lucy felt as if she'd been underwater for hours when she finally emerged from the sedative flowing into her veins. She knew by the smell and sounds that she was in a hospital. It took her a while to recall that Calum had been there. Her gaze lingered on the window ledge with cards and a moth orchid plant.

She remembered him talking to her. Most of what he'd said she'd forgotten, yet what she couldn't forget was his admission that he loved her, and his loving had nothing to do with the baby. Reaching over, she pressed the call button for the nurses' station.

A middle-aged woman in scrubs entered the room. "Good morning."

Lucy ran her free hand through her mussed hair. "Good morning. When will it be possible for me to go home?"

"Your doctor will be here in a couple of hours, and if she signs off on your discharge, then you can leave. Do you have someone that can pick you up?"

"Yes, she does," Calum said as he walked into the room. "I've already spoken to Dr. Ramos, and she said the patient is cleared to go home." He handed the nurse the discharge paper. He placed a small, quilted bag on a chair. "I brought you some clothes."

Lucy bit her lower lip when she met his eyes. It was obvious he hadn't bothered to shave and the stubble along with the goatee made him even more ruggedly handsome. He was there for her, just like he'd promised to be. It meant everything to her.

She raised her right hand, drawing attention to the IV. "Can you please remove this so I can shower and get dressed?"

"Don't worry about showering, bae. You can do that at home," Calum said quietly.

"After I check with your doctor I'll remove the IV. After that someone will bring a wheelchair for you," the nurse said.

Lucy smiled. "Thank you so much."

Five minutes later the nurse returned and removed the needle, covered the spot with gauze and then tape. Calum waited until the nurse left, closing the door, to help Lucy out of the hospital gown and into her street clothes. "Do you want to take the cards?"

"Yes." She'd planned to send thank-you greetings to those who had sent them." She kissed his jaw. "I know the plant is from you."

"Really?"

"You should know that you're not that subtle."

He smiled. "Neither are you, don't forget." He helped Lucy to stand. "How do you feel?"

She tested her balance. "I'm okay."

There came a knock on the door and an orderly came in with a wheelchair. Lucy sat and the man pushed her down the hallway to the nurses' station, Calum following. He signed the papers confirming he was taking responsibility for her.

The sun was high in the sky when she sat beside him as he drove toward Spring Forest.

"Thank you, Calum."

"For what?"

"For taking care of me."

"I thought that was understood, Lucy. No matter what, I will take care of you and the baby. I hope what happened a few days ago was enough for you to trust me enough to be true to my word."

"I do trust you."

He gave her a quick sidelong glance before returning his gaze to the road. "Thank you."

"I trust you *and* I love you."

"I already know that. You admitted that the night you walked out of my house mad as a wet hen."

Lucy's jaw dropped. She'd been so incensed that she didn't remember telling him that. "I can recall you telling me that you loved me."

His eyebrows lifted. "When was that, Lucy Tucker?"

"When I was juiced up and you thought I was asleep. I distinctly remember you saying that you loved me, and that I was the most precious thing in your life. And that your loving me had nothing to do with our baby."

"Well, damn," he swore under his breath. "Did I really say all that?"

"Don't dare play dumb, Mr. Total Recall Ramsey. Yeah, you did."

"Guilty as charged." Slowing at a stop sign, Calum winked at her. "Now that we've gotten our true confessions out of the way, I think it's time we start planning other things."

"What other things, Calum?"

"What color do you want to paint the walls in the nursery?"

Lucy successful hid her disappointment behind a too bright smile. She'd thought Calum was going to talk about setting a date for when they would eventually marry. "I'm leaning toward seafoam green."

"That's nice."

They arrived at her house and Calum assisted her out of the SUV and unlocked the front door. Silence greeted her. It was the first time in a very long time there wasn't the sound of Buttercup or her puppies.

She didn't protest when Calum helped her out of her clothes, then undressed himself and got into the shower with her to shampoo her hair and wash her body. If this was what he meant by taking care of her, then Lucy was all in.

He spent the day with her, making certain she ate, and when he left, she felt as if she'd lost a part of herself. She loved him just that much.

After a few days of rest, Lucy felt she was going stir-crazy and decided it was time for her to go back to the bookstore. She needed something to get her mind off the fact that even though Calum had stopped by every day to bring her lunch, and then every evening so they could share dinner, he hadn't volunteered to sleep over. She was reluctant to ask why.

She unlocked the door to Chapter One and turned on the air-conditioning. The store had been closed for the weekend and the buildup of heat was stifling.

Lucy had just turned over the open sign when

Ms. Fowler walked in. She was surprised when the woman hugged her.

"How are you feeling?"

"I'm good."

"Evelyn and I had a little meeting the other day and we both decided you're not to lift anything whatsoever until the baby is born. If you do, then you'll find yourself looking for two assistants to replace us."

"You would quit?"

"Yes."

"I can't believe I'm being blackmailed by my own employees," Lucy said under her breath.

The bell chimed and Miss Grace walked in. "Well, look at you, missy. Welcome back."

"I told her if she dares to lift a box, we're going to quit."

"Angela's right. If you give us a scare again, I'm outta here. You've no right to do that to yourself— or to your sweet boyfriend. Whenever we asked him how you were doing, he would get very emotional. You really scared him."

Ms. Fowler placed her handbag in a file drawer under the counter. "He's such a fine young man, Lucy."

"Oh, really? When did you become best friends?"

"When I realized he loved you enough to drop everything when you nearly passed out. The man adores you, and if you're too blind to see that, then you don't deserve him. If my daughter wasn't married, I definitely would try and hook her up with him."

Lucy put up a hand. "Stop it, Miss Grace. You don't need to worry about setting him up with anyone, because I'm not leaving Calum."

She walked to her office and sat down at the workstation. It seemed so lonely without any dogs. The thought had just popped into her head when she heard a familiar bark. Lucy couldn't stop smiling when Buttercup raced in, tail wagging.

She went to her knees and hugged the dog's neck. "What are you doing here? You look marvelous with your new collar." Then she noticed the handwritten note attached to the collar.

Lucy barely realized her hand was shaking when she read the note: *Buttercup belongs to Lucy and Calum Ramsey.*

She started laughing and couldn't stop at the same time Calum walked into the office, cupping a hand under her elbow and helping her to her feet. "It was the best proposal I could think of. If we're going to have a baby together, then why not also have a dog we both love so much? You can't imagine how much I love you and our baby, and you will make me the happiest man in the world if you'd agree to be my wife."

Lucy wrapped both arms around his neck and

kissed him. He'd adopted Buttercup. "Yes to both," she whispered against his mouth.

She hadn't known when she'd relocated to Spring Forest to start over she would get a full-circle family that included a husband, dog *and* a baby. But she couldn't be happier with how things had turned out.

Calum kicked the door shut, picked her up, settled her on the workstation and kissed her until Lucy reminded him of where they were.

He pulled back and winked at her. "To be continued."

And Lucy knew it would continue for many more years to come.

* * * * *

COMING NEXT MONTH FROM

⊕ HARLEQUIN

SPECIAL EDITION

#2911 FINDING FORTUNE'S SECRET

The Fortunes of Texas: The Wedding Gift • by Allison Leigh

Stefan Mendoza has found Justine Maloney in Texas nearly a year after their whirlwind Miami romance. Now that he's learned he's a father, he wants to "do the right thing." But for Justine, marriage without love is a deal breaker. And simmering below the surface is a family secret that could change everything for them both—forever...

#2912 BLOOM WHERE YOU'RE PLANTED

The Friendship Chronicles • by Darby Baham

Jennifer Pritchett feels increasingly left behind as her friends move on to the next steps in their lives. As she goes to therapy to figure out how to bloom in her own right, her boyfriend, Nick Carrington, finds himself being the one left behind. Can they each get what they need out of this relationship? Or will the flowers shrivel up before they do?

#2913 THE TRIPLETS' SECRET WISH

Lockharts Lost & Found • by Cathy Gillen Thacker

Emma Lockhart and Tom Reid were each other's one true love—until their dueling ambitions drove them apart. Now Emma has an opportunity that could bring the success she craves. When Tom offers his assistance in exchange for her help with his triplets, Emma can't resist the cowboy's pull on her heart. Maybe her real success lies in taking a chance on happily-ever-after...

#2914 A STARLIGHT SUMMER

Welcome to Starlight • by Michelle Major

When eight-year-old Anna Johnson asked Ella Samuelson for help in fixing up her father with a new wife, Ella only agreed because she knew the child and her father had been through the wringer. Too bad she found herself drawn to the handsome and kind single dad!

#2915 THE LITTLE MATCHMAKER

Top Dog Dude Ranch • by Catherine Mann

Working at the Top Dog Dude Ranch is ideal for contractor Micah Fuller as he learns to parent his newly adopted nephew. But school librarian Susanna Levine's insistence that young Benji needs help reading has Micah overwhelmed. Hiring Susanna as Benji's tutor seems perfect...until Benji starts matchmaking. Micah would give his nephew anything, but getting himself a wife? A feat considering Susanna is adamant about keeping their relationship strictly business.

#2916 LOVE OFF THE LEASH

Furever Yours • by Tara Taylor Quinn

When Pets for Vets volunteer pilot Greg Martin's plane goes down after transporting a dog, coordinator Wendy Alvarez is filled with guilt. She knows a service dog will help, but Greg's just too stubborn. If Wendy can get him to "foster" Jedi, she's certain his life will be forever altered. She just never expected hers to change, as well.

YOU CAN FIND MORE INFORMATION ON UPCOMING HARLEQUIN TITLES,
FREE EXCERPTS AND MORE AT HARLEQUIN.COM.

HSECNM0422

*Mariella Jacob was one of the world's premier bridal
designers. One viral PR disaster later, she's trying to
get her torpedoed career back on track in small-town
Magnolia, North Carolina. With a second-hand store
and a new business venture helping her friends turn the
Wildflower Inn into a wedding venue, Mariella is
finally putting at least one mistake behind her.
Until that mistake—in the glowering, handsome
form of Alex Ralsten—moves to Magnolia too...*

Read on for a sneak preview of
Wedding Season,
the next book in USA TODAY *bestselling author
Michelle Major's Carolina Girls series!*

"You still don't belong here." Mariella crossed her arms
over her chest, and Alex commanded himself not to notice
her body, perfect as it was.

"That makes two of us, and yet here we are."

"I was here first," she muttered. He'd heard the argument
before, but it didn't sway him.

"You're not running me off, Mariella. I needed a fresh
start, and this is the place I've picked for my home."

"My plan was to leave the past behind me. You are a
physical reminder of so many mistakes I've made."

"I can't say that upsets me too much," he lied. It didn't
make sense, but he hated that he made her so uncomfortable.
Hated even more that sometimes he'd purposely drive by

her shop to get a glimpse of her through the picture window. Talk about a glutton for punishment.

She let out a low growl. "You are an infuriating man. Stubborn and callous. I don't even know if you have a heart."

"Funny." He kept his voice steady even as memories flooded him, making his head pound. "That's the rationale Amber gave me for why she cheated with your fiancé. My lack of emotions pushed her into his arms. What was his excuse?"

She looked out at the street for nearly a minute, and Alex wondered if she was even going to answer. He followed her gaze to the park across the street, situated in the center of the town. There were kids at the playground and several families walking dogs on the path that circled the perimeter. Magnolia was the perfect place to raise a family.

If a person had the heart to be that kind of a man—the type who married the woman he loved and set out to be a good husband and father. Alex wasn't cut out for a family, but he liked it in the small coastal town just the same.

"I was too committed to my job," she said suddenly and so quietly he almost missed it.

"Ironic since it was your job that introduced him to Amber."

"Yeah." She made a face. "This is what I'm talking about, Alex. A past I don't want to revisit."

"Then stay away from me, Mariella," he advised. "Because I'm not going anywhere."

"Then maybe I will," she said and walked away.

Don't miss
Wedding Season *by Michelle Major,*
available May 2022 wherever
HQN books and ebooks are sold.